Syracuse Browning Club

Memorial Meeting of the Syracuse Browning Club

held at May memorial church, Syracuse, N.Y., January 9, 1890

Syracuse Browning Club

Memorial Meeting of the Syracuse Browning Club
held at May memorial church, Syracuse, N.Y., January 9, 1890

ISBN/EAN: 9783337285166

Printed in Europe, USA, Canada, Australia, Japan

Cover: Foto ©Andreas Hilbeck / pixelio.de

More available books at **www.hansebooks.com**

—OF THE—

SYRACUSE BROWNING CLUB,

—HELD AT—

May Memorial Church, Syracuse, N. Y.,
January 9, 1890.

SYRACUSE, N. Y.:

C. W. BARDEEN, PUBLISHER,

1890.

The Syracuse Browning Club is the oldest in America, having been organized Oct. 28, 1882, and held weekly meetings exc t in the summer, ever since. The number of members is nomi ally limited to fifty, but has usually been permitted somewhat ·o exceed that limit. The meetings have been held on Thursday afternoons, from three to five, in addition to which there have been occasional evening entertainments, with lectures by such men as Canon Farrar and Prof. Corson. The general plan of the regular meetings has been to read consecutively some volume of the author's works, enough being assigned for an afternoon to occupy perhaps a fourth of the time, the rest being given to discussion not only of the thought of the poet but also of the principles involved. It has therefore often happened that the meetings had quite as much an ethical as a literary character.

A small library of various editions of Browning's Works has been built up by purchase from time to time, and is at present deposited with the Central Library. A list of the volumes now on hand is given on the following pages.

LIBRARY OF THE SYRACUSE BROWNING CLUB.

The following volumes are carefully described in "A Bibliography of Robert Browning, from 1833 to 1881. Compiled by Frederick J. Furnivall. Second Edition, 8vo, pp. 95, London, 1881." The number prefixed to a title shows the first appearance of the poem, and the chronological order in which it appeared. A number in parenthesis indicates the page in the Bibliography on which the book is described.

1. *Pauline;* a Fragment of a Confession. Pp. 71. London, 1833. *Facsimile reprint*, London, 1886.

2. *Paracelsus.* Pp. xi, 216. London, 1835.

5. *Strafford:* an historical Tragedy. Pp. vi, 131. London, 1837.

6. *Sordello.* Pp. iv, 253. London, 1840.

(P. 51) *Poems.* In two volumes. A new edition. Pp. viii, 386. London, 1849.

53. *Christmas-Eve and Easter-Day.* A Poem. Pp. iv, 142. London, 1850.

(P. 53) *Men and Women.* In two volumes. Pp. iv, 260; iv, 241. London, 1855.

107–123. *Dramatis Personae.* Pp. vi, 250. London, 1864.

(P. 62) *The Poetical Works* of Robert Browning, M. A., Honorary Fellow of Balliol College, Oxford. In six volumes, pp. viii, 310; iv, 287; iii, 305; iv, 310; iv, 321; iv, 233. London, 1868.

126. *The Ring and the Book.* In four volumes, pp. 74, 72, 89, 92. London, 1868.

129. *Prince Hohenstiel Schwangau, Saviour of Society.* Pp. iv, 148. London, 1871.

130. *Fifine at the Fair.* Pp. xii, 171. London, 1872.

131. *Red Cotton Night-Cap Country, or Turf and Towers.* Pp. vi, 282. London, 1873.

132. *Aristophanes' Apology, including a Transcript from Euripides, being the Last Adventure of Balaustion.* Pp. viii, 366. London, 1875.

133. *The Inn Album.* Pp. iv, 211. London, 1875.

135–151. *Pacchiarotto, and how he worked in Distemper: with other Poems.* Pp. viii, 241. London, 1876.

152. *The Agamemnon of Æschylus, transcribed by Robert Browning.* Pp. xi, 148. London, 1877.

153. *La Saisiaz; The Two Poets of Croisic.* Pp. viii, 201. London, 1878.

156–161. *Dramatic Idyls.* Pp. vi, 143. London, 1879.

162–169, *Dramatic Idyls. Second Series.* Pp. viii, 149. London, 1880.

(P. 76) Moxon's Miniature Poets. A Selection from the works of Robert Browning. London, 1865.

Also the following later volumes:

Jocoseria, London, 1883.

Ferishtah's Fancies, London, 1884.

Parleyings with Certain People, London, 1887.

Asolando, London, 1890.

Poetical Works, 10 vol., London, 1888.

Poetic and Dramatic Works, 6 vols., Boston, 1887.

———

Horse and Foot, or Pilgrims to Parnassus, Richard Crawley, London, 1868.

Essays on Robert Browning's Poetry, John T. Nettleship, London, 1868.

Stories from Robert Browning, Fredk. May Holland, London, 1882.

Golden thoughts from the Spiritual Guide of Migall Molinos, Preface by J. H. Shorthouse, London, 1883.

Handbook to the Works of Robert Browning, Mrs. Sutherland Orr, London, 1885.

Introduction to the Study of Robert Browning, Hiram Corson, LL. D., Boston, 1886.

Introduction to the Study of Browning, Arthur Symons, London, 1886.

Browning's Women, Mary E. Burt and E. E. Hale, Chicago, 1886.

Christmas-Eve and Easter-Day and other Poems, Heloise E. Hersey and Wm. J. Rolfe, Boston, 1886.

Select Poems of Robert Browning, Wm. J. Rolfe and Heloise E. Hersey, N. Y., 1887.

Studies in the Poetry of Robert Browning, James Fotheringham, London, 1887.

———

PREVIOUS PUBLICATIONS OF THE SYRACUSE BROWNING CLUB.

———

1. The Constitution of the Syracuse Browning Club, with a Sketch of the Organization, and its List of Members. 8vo, pp. 8, Syracuse, 1882.

2. The Syracuse Browning Club. Brief Abstract of the Minutes of Seventy Meetings, with Two Papers by Mrs. James L. Bagg. 8vo, pp. 20, Syracuse, 1885.

[The two papers by Mrs. Bagg are " Interpretation of Childe " Roland," read at the 34th meeting of the Club, Nov. 18, 1883; and "Eglamor and Sordello," read at the 62d meeting of the Club, Dec. 17, 1884.].

CONTENTS.

❧ A Meeting of the ❧

Syracuse Browning Club

In Memory of

ROBERT BROWNING,

Died in Venice, Dec. 12, 1889.

May Memorial Church, Thursday, Jan. 9, 1890.

❧ PROGRAMME ❧

Browning as a Historian......................Rev. Chas. J. Little, D. D.

Browning as a Help to Living..........................Mrs. J. L. Bagg.

Browning as a Religious Teacher............... .....Rev. E. W. Mundy.

Reading—Prospice..................................Mrs. E. H. Merrell.

Browning as an Artist..................................Mr. E. H. Merrell.

Browning as a Philosopher...................Miss Arria S. Huntington.

Browning as a Dramatist...........................Rev. S. R. Calthrop.

Some of Browning's Beliefs...........................Mr. C. W. Bardeen.

Reading—The Grammarian's Funeral.................Mrs. R. H. Davis.

BROWNING'S USE OF HISTORY.

Browning and Tennyson have published verse chiefly, and History as ordinarily written is essentially prose. Indeed the first appearance of prose in literature is where the epic and lyric break down to quiet narrative, when Homer makes room for Herodotus and Æschylus for Thucydides. A poet's treatment of history must therefore be judged by the canons of his art. He creates for us a life or an epoch, illuminating some coil and cluster of human activities by the rhythmic speech which discloses to us motive and emotion and reveals the hidden laws of being, from which there is for none of us, escape.

Hence to the poet, the past is either like the valley of dry bones into which Ezekiel came, the breath of life upon his lips, or a world of mere suggestions out of which he shapes images, which corresponding exactly to no realities of history are yet ofter truer than the unilluminated fact; more truthful just as certain experiments of the laboratory are more truthful than the phenomena of nature unassisted, in that they bring us nearer to the laws for which all science seeks.

Now in his treatment of historic fact Mr. Browning was both prophet and creator. Sometimes, for instance in *King Victor and King Charles* he simply raised forgotten dead to life; sometimes in the glow of his powerful mind the miracle of the fiery furnace is wrought before our eyes and there appears a form nobler and diviner than any committed to the flames. Balaustion for example is such an apparition amid the realities of ruined Athens; an apparition serenely (why should I shrink from the Hellenic word), divinely beautiful. And only by her

intervention is it possible for the Poet to place Aristophanes before us in a radiance sufficient to disclose the startling convolu-
tions of his character.   This poetic glorification of historic fact
compares with the dull and lustreless chronicle as the diamond
compares with the common forms of carbon; this is fact
wrought to its highest potency, no longer inert and opaque but
alive with light and flashing with ever new suggestion.

When Mr. Browning aimed at reproduction merely, he spared
no pains to discover the exact reality; musty chronicles and forgotten memoirs were studied with antiquarian zest and every detail noted.   But his interest in history was in the disclosure and
development of character; to use his own words he counted
nothing worthy of study but the incidents in the history of a
soul.   Yet he was too great a scholar, too deep a thinker, and
too much the child of his age not to perceive the correlation of
souls, the imprisonment of men in their environment, the clash
of individual life with stubborn and hostile circumstance; too
great an artist not to take advantage of the immense variety of
back-ground which history would furnish for his men and
women, caught in the hour and article of self-revelation.

So we have Italy presented in *Sordello*, in *Luria*, in the *Soul's
Tragedy*, in the *Ring and the Book;* Athens and Hellenic life
in *Balaustion* and *Aristophanes* with a richness of detail, a fulness of learning, a minuteness of erudite knowledge which sur-
prises and delights, and all held, for the most part, in due subor-
dination to the characters which live and move before us.

Strafford is remarkable for the care bestowed upon each person
of the drama; Paracelsus on the other hand for the skill with
which the heart of the real man's mystery has been plucked out
and glorified.   In the English play all that could heighten the
spectator's interest in character or plot has been discovered and
made use of; if it fails to be history illuminated and transformed as a historic drama ought to be, it is because the central
figures are hardly of colossal mould.   Yet possibly it is the per-

spective of the historian which makes them seem so great and the Poet has after all, only reduced them to life size.

Mr. Browning has been cosmopolitan and catholic in his selec-tion of historical characters, and singularly free from bias and prejudice of every kind. And there again the Poet proves him-self more truthful than the partisan historian. Take for in-stance Mr. Browning's delineation of Italian character and contrast it with the paradox expounded so brilliantly in Lord Macaulay's Essay upon Machiavelli. The land of Dante and Vittoria Colonna, of Manzoni and Silvio Pellico and Mazzini has found no nobler defence than in the immortal picture of An-tonio Pignatelli, called Innocent XII. Though I must speak with hesitation here, since the Encyclopedia Britannica refers to Mr. Browning's portrait as a truthful and powerful sketch of Innocent XI., who was quite another man, though also great and good. For all that, the sketch is a faithful portrait of a great and pious pope who lived a very noble life and stood for Christ among his fellow-men. Mr. Browning himself spoke too much per-haps through his characters, making them give his thought rather than their own; he possesses them when he ought to be possessed by them: a defect which is especially noticeable in a character taken from the historic world. But making every abatement which the truth requires, one may say without extravagance that no writer of our age has known more about the men and times of which he gave us pictures. Again there are indications everywhere but especially in the minor poems, of a knowledge, rich and various of which his published work is only the outer crust, however rich in precious things. Who that studies the picture of Napoleon given us in the *Incident in the French Camp* does not wish that we had a Napoleon in Exile by the same master hand? But it was characteristic of Mr. Browning to shun the over-treated figures of history. These did not seem to him to be the makers of epochs after all. "God's "puppets best and worst are we; there are no last nor first."

This truth so deeply felt by him kept his thoughts from popular idols and inspired him to the representation of the nobly done and ignobly forgotten, of the bravely suffered and inadequately praised. Like Carlyle he had a quick mind for the anecdote which discloses the nature of a soul; and knew how to seize and shape it into enduring form. He did not always hunt these to their sources, that he might verify them. Nor was he as poet bound to. But the number of these allusions is legion and they break out everywhere. Right in the midst of the *Statue and the Bust* leaps out a passage from an ancient chronicle; *Peter of Abano* closes with a story from Suetonius never dreamed worth quoting till Browning saw its deep significance. Chronicle and memoir were fluent in his mind, or rather floated in fragments to be poured out with the molten thought.

Finally let me note that though Mr. Browning attempted in the maturity of his powers, the delineation of a great epoch only once, he achieved it perfectly. The Rome of Innocent XII. hardly gave him a great epoch; Strafford was an earlier work and Sordello a resolute and wilful struggle with the impossible. But *Aristophanes' Apology* is more nearly the Athens of the Peloponnesian War than Schiller's William Tell is the Switzerland of Gessler. And how vastly more difficult the task of the English poet. How easy to describe the hunters and shepherds of the Alps! How bewildering the varied strength and splendor of Hellenic life! Nor is the picture surface merely. Pictorial history here becomes reflective and philosophical. That which is elsewhere expressed dimly in hints and glints, shines forth here without obstructing cloud. The poet with a subtlety that Carneades might envy defends but does not exculpate the great comedian; extenuates but will not justify; holds him as appointed leader to the task of leadership; demands of him conduct steadied by his conscience, and traces with a master thinker's craft the ruin of the city to " the pipings and dancings, the greetings and the guzzling " which Aristophanes was fain to believe could " build Athenai to the "skies once more."

" For the very day Euripides was born
" Those flute girls—Phaps-Elaphion at their head—
" Did blow their best, did dance their worst, the while
" Sparté pulled down the walls, wrecked wide the work,
" Laid low each merest molehill of defence,
" And so the Power, Athenai, passed away ! "

But this crash of Athens into an immortal wreck—
Who has told it for us with wiser comment or in a nobler strain ?

CHARLES J. LITTLE.

AID TO LIVING FROM BROWNING.

This many-sided poet has also his practical side, his deep concern being to present a "theory of life," and to offer a gospel which reconciles to life's insoluble problems. Taking the world as it is, and asking of it not more than it can give, "he dwells ever in a high calm." His philosophy makes impossible frantic activities, Quixotic crusades, and hysteric wails. Always we are reminded that to-day's mis-carriage and pain issues in to-morrow's wisdom. To be patient and to be calm must be the mood of the optimist.

Browning's view of the nature of man is based upon a wide study of individual man and of the race, in their successive stages of development from animal, through the rational, moral and spiritual. Man is many natured. All faculties of his being have their rights, the delights of sound, sight, touch, taste, beauty, reverie, imagination, poetic and spiritual ecstacy,—all help each, and each helps all to the harmonious development of the complete man; so may the earth-man live the earth-life with due recognition of the spiritual nature, and the spiritual man live the spiritual life with due recognition of the earthly nature. Browning emphasizes the value, significance, dignity, and rights of flesh. Body is soul's tool, agent, medium, through which come man's experience; it is soul's aid or hinderance, and soul's shield and pleasure house. And "pleasant is the flesh." The joy of physical existence is jubilantly chanted in David's song before Saul,

"How good is man's life, the mere living! How fit to employ
"All the heart, and the soul, and the senses, forever in joy!
"Oh! our manhood's prime vigor!"
(14)

" Let us not always say, 'spite of this flesh I strove, made head,
" gained ground upon the whole.'   As the bird wings and sings,
" let us cry ;—'all good things are ours, nor soul helps flesh more,
" now, than flesh helps soul.' "

He who accords all honor and reverence to man's body, may
be expected to insist on the sanctity of things near ; and our poet
mourns that "too much life here has been walled about with
" disgrace." He would have a man, a man while here, " with all
" his heart and soul throwing himself on the present." Wait
for some trancendent life reserved by Fate to follow this? O!
never ! " Life here and now, gives ample opportunity for all
" manly, brave and beneficent beginnings." It is " no mean stage
" too narrow for our wide performance ; "—we are too little to
enact the parts we are able to conceive. " Where is the man
" who has shown himself too great for earth and human life, with
" its many and complex needs ? "

A noble conception of life's consummation should save from
contempt its beginning. Earthly experiences are not simply to
be tolerated, endured,—they are the dignified ; and as " God
" joys in the uncouth joy of the incomplete world, so man may
" take a pleasure in his

> " Half reasons, faint aspirings, dim
> " Struggles for truth, his poorest fallacies,
> " Prejudice, and fears, and cares, and doubts,
> " Which all touch on nobleness despite
> " Their error ; all tend upwardly, though weak,
> " Like plants in mines which never saw the sun,
> " But dream of him, and guess where he may be,
> " And do their best to climb and get to him."

Man's concern is with *to-day*.   To live overmuch in the future
is to sacrifice the present and so peril that future ; as unwise as
to " wear furry garments in Italy in preparation for a residence
" in Russia." Man loses the joy that belongs to the physical
when he attempts to discount the delights of the spiritual. Our

poet enjoins to be satisfied with earth's knowledge, experiences
and insights, leaving for the next life the lessons that can be
learned there only. " It is not for man to snatch fire from heaven.
"Earthly lamps, and so much fire as sun vouchsafes, he may
" have to walk by."

> " And what is this life's purpose?
> " To learn earth first, discover Will, Power, Love,
> " Below, then seek law's confirmation above."

On earth *begins* man's spiritual evolution. This is not a world
of finalities. The perfect life of the spirit is not attainable here,
and the absolute religious truth is not attainable here. Man's
approximations to absolute truth, his creeds and formulations are
as tabernacles,—never homes. Every *living* soul outgrows the
spiritual house it has built,—its successive shelters being but for
a night's tarry on the journey of many stops and many starts and
no arrival.

And of life's activities, the poet says, " To live and learn, not
" first learn and then live, is our concern ; to act to-day, learning
"thereby to act to-morrow." To tarry for fulness of love, or
completeness of knowledge, or perfectness in aim is to "see never
"the time and the place." *This* is life's business ;—with
to-day's rude tool and to-day's awkward hand to do to-day's
common task. To-morrow brings the sharper tool, the nimbler
hand and the grander work. Browning has little patience with
the inert, the supine, the procrastinating. He has all patience
with crudity in the statue, coarseness in the picture, unripeness in
the thought, clumsiness in the deed, so these be the expression of
the artificer's highest ideal. " Trusting his feeble, fullest sense,"
he would have " man contend to the uttermost for his life's set
" prize, be it what it will ; for the sin of each frustrate ghost is
" the unlit lamp and the ungirt loin." " So shall the soul declare
" itself by the thing it does. Be hate that fruit or love that
" fruit, it forwards the general deed of man ; and each of the
" many, helps to recruit the life of the race by a general plan ;
" each living his own to boot." " Thus man works his proper

" nature out, and ascertains his rank and final place ; " and " just
" the creature he was bound to be, he will *become*, nor thwart at
"all God's purpose in creation."

Of man's work, the poet asks

> " So, all men strive and who succeeds?
> " Look at the end of work, contrast
> " The petty Done, the Undone vast,
> " This present with the hopeful past.
> " What hand and brain went ever paired?
> " What heart, alike conceived and dared ?
> " What act proved all its thought had been ?
> " What will but felt the fleshly screen ? "

" Yet the will's somewhat ! " " A man's reach should be beyond
" his grasp " : and " if this life gave all, what were there to look
"forward to ? " Earth is the place for attempt—"anon per-
"formance." And this "stops my despair. 'Tis not what man
"does, that exalts him, but what he would do." "What I
" aspired to be, and was not, comforts me ; a brute I might have
"been, but would not sink in the scale." And so, " I live, go
"through the world, try, prove, reject, prefer, still struggling to
" effect my warfare ; happy that I can be thwarted as a man ;
" not left in God's contempt apart, with ghastly smooth life, dead
" at heart."

Who shall say of his fellow, "he has failed " ?

> "That low man seeks a little thing to do,
> " Sees it and does it ;
> " This high man with a great thing to pursue,
> " Dies ere he knows it.
> "That, has the world here—
> "This, throws himself on God, and unperplexed,
> " Seeking, shall find Him ;
> " God's task, to make the heavenly period
> " Perfect the earthen."

What is success and what failure ?

" Now who shall arbitrate ?
" Ten men love what I hate,
" Shun what I follow, slight what I receive :
" Ten who in eyes and ears
" Match me ; they all surmise,
" They, this thing, and I that,
" Whom shall my soul believe ? "—

for " our human speech is naught, our testimony false, our fame
" and human estimation, words and wind." Men's standards differ each from each, and all differ from the absolute and unknown
standard by which lives might be rightly judged. Then too,
men never gather all the facts. It has been said that, " this life
" being but a small part of life, men should know of the rest be-
" fore they can say of this portion, that it is failure or success."
The perfect judgment waits God's time, who knows all from the
beginning. Man, who " sees light, half shine, half shade," looks
" to the size of things done that have their price here," the vul-
gar mass called work ; the low world can value in a trice, plumb
with its coarse thumb ; God holds appraising in his hollow palm,
the seed of act, thoughts hardly to be packed into a narrow act,
fancies that broke through language and escaped ; all instincts
immature, all purposes unsure, that weighed not as his work,
yet swelled the man's account. "All he could never be, all men
" ignored, this was he worth to God whose wheel the pitcher
" shaped."

For the deformed, idiotic, stunted, limp, and ignorant, whom
men call " foolish," Browning has infinite patience and hope ;
all are backward scholars waiting the Great Teacher. And
for the hateful, noxious, the morally insane whom men call
" wicked," he has infinite patience and hope,—for the little half-
completed castaway who was so much worse than herself; for " Ot-
" tima, the temptress, magnificent in sin "; for Guido, chief of
villains,—all wait the " touch of God's shadow wherein is heal-
" ing." The worst man has something that links him on to
humanity, " some germ of good, that may grow to choke out the

" poisonous, rank growth of a life-time." Quickening, soul-kindling, conversion " may, will come to all, by God's own ways " occult." Some suddenness of fate may cleave the flesh, give issue to the spirit birth: some lightning-stroke may cure the blind; God's spear may pierce a window in the soul, whence the imprisoned flash shall leap and find itself at one with God's own sun—" Else I avert my face, nor penetrate into that sad, ob-" scure, sequestered place, where God unmakes, but to remake " the soul, he else made first in vain."

And has *earth* no hope for such ? Elisha raised the dead—" a " credible feat enough," our poet says, " Man may not *create*,—" he may *restore;* a virgin wick he cannot light, the almost-" dead lamp he may relume."

> " Such men are even now upon the earth,
> " Serene amid the half-formed creatures round,
> " Who should be saved by them, and joined with them."

Through Christ-like souls is " man born from above," or through higher personality ; and through such souls alone, God stooping shows sufficient of His light for us in the dark to rise by. " By him, shall man be ' lifted to his level,' " made cognizant of the mas-er," see his true " function revealed," and " be admitted to a fellowship with the soul of things."

In a world of failure, loss, pain, decay and imperfection, our poet finds sufficient consolation for life as it is, and for man as he is, in the thought that " man is made to grow, not stop ; " " what " comes to perfection perishes : " " what's whole can increase no " more, is dwarfed and dies, since here's its sphere." " Progress " is man's distinction, man's alone, not God's and not the beasts. " God is, they are,—man partly is, and wholly hopes to be."

> " God's gift is that man shall conceive of truth,
> " And yearn to gain it, catching at mistake,
> " As midway help till he reach fact indeed."

Every sorrow, loss and pain yields "increase of knowledge, "since he learns because he lives, which is to be a man, set to "instruct himself by his past self." Rejoice, "that man is hurled "from change to change unceasingly, his soul's wings never furled."

What end to the striving? "To reach the ultimate, angel's law, "indulging every instinct of the soul, there, where law, life, joy, "impulse are one thing."

MARY E. BAGG.

BROWNING AS A THEOLOGIAN.

In the study of Browning the chief thing is not criticism or defence of his teachings, but a careful understanding of what he has to say. And it is difficult, if not impossible, to understand a man who is on a level above the student. It is specially difficult to be entirely fair in questions of theology, because theology is so related to religion that thought and feeling are both involved. And while the attractiveness of feeling is in the local or personal color which it gives to thought, that attraction causes the needle of truth to vary from its accuracy of direction.

But beyond this, it is to be said of Browning that he is not a theologian and therefore has not a theology. He is a deeply religious poet. His entire writings all full of religious thought and feeling. A theologian is a logician. Browning is a poet, a seer. He is comprehensive. He embraces everything in his vision and in his description. There is nothing of the exclusiveness of the theologian in his utterances. As to the artist, so to him, everything is of interest and service. He lays the entire universe under contribution to his page. He seems to see, as it is said in Genesis the creator saw, that all things are good. He believes in everything. The one passport to his favor is that a thing is.

There is no scientific theological statement possible of the system of such a writer. You can prove anything from him. He seems to have learned what Emerson teaches, that the whole truth is not spoken until the opposite has been affirmed. It is impossible for a logical system to hold contradictory statements. Seers always speak contradictions. Hence there are numberless opinions concerning Browning's theology. In that regard, how-

(21)

ever, he shares the fate of many clear-seeing men and of the writers of the New Testament.

Browning seems to hold the fundamental doctrines of christianity, and to interpret them as the eternal principles of existence. While he accepts the christian theology he makes all truths to be of universal application. He is properly a christian because he believes in God, believes in the Incarnation and believes in Immortality. The poems *Christmas Eve, Easter-Day, Saul,* and others teach these doctrines with great distinctness.

But these christian doctrines are not held by Browning in the narrow and exclusive fashion of any church or sect. They are in his statement of them thoroughly inclusive. His Incarnation is not an event in which the divine power or the divine love is *exhausted.* The divine power, and the divine love were before the historical Incarnation, are now, and ever shall be. Christ is not merely the divine form, he is the divine qualities.

Or possibly it would more clearly state Browning's thought to say that the Incarnation is to him not a solitary fact putting God into a new relation with his creation, but that it is a fact which illustrates the eternal relation of God to the Universe. He seems to think that it was not an expedient devised to remedy a defect, but that it is one exemplification of the permanent relation of God to all things.

As a consequence of this view, he says little of the historic Incarnation. Christ to him is the God in human form who was such from the beginning and ever shall be such. In his essay on Shelly, Browning says that Shelly accepted christianity but denied its historic bases. It might be said of Browning that he accepts christianity, but gives little attention to its historic bases.

His doctrine of Immortality seems in like manner to be no artificial system of adjustments, no mechanical arrangement of pleasures and pains, but the eternal order of things, insured to us not by promises and statutes, but by the nature of existence, by the necessities of the divine love.

Browning's idea of God seems to be that he is all-powerful, all-wise, and all-good.   And in such a supreme he finds assurance of the excellence of all that is.   He believes therefore in the universe, he is wholly at ease concerning the origin, present state, and destiny of all persons and things, he sees that love and wisdom are everywhere and he is therefore content.   To him God is " all and in all."   Hence to him every atom and every person of the universe is essential to the universe and performs its function in the universe.   Popes, priests, saints, fair women, brave men, cowards, hypocrites, murderers, princes, beggars, thieves, every human being seems to appeal equally to his careful interest.   He gives such attention to the imperfect in life that one able critic characterizes him as the master of the grotesque in poetry.*

The opposites good and evil, pleasure and pain, holiness and sin, the finite and infinite seem in his thought to be but different aspects of the same thing.   Opposites to him make one.   With such perceptions, the old theological problems vanish, all life is one, and Browning regards existence not as a critic to judge it but as a seer to observe it.   E. W. MUNDY.

---

* See Bagehot on " Wordsworth, Tennyson and Browning."

BROWNING AS AN ARTIST.

"The course of Nature is the art of God."

"In ancient days the name of prophet and of poet[1] was the "same."

Browning though of exceeding fertility and versatility of genius, and so profoundly acquainted with the history, and sympathetic with the development of every fine art as to have obtained intuition of its origin, motive and function, and prescience of its future, was yet not like Buonarotti, poet, painter, sculptor, architect, and statesman all in one, nor, though musician, was he composer. His only art was the art *par excellence*, and even in this his productive activity did not extend to its every branch.

Wherefore in speaking of him as artist, productions belonging to diverse spheres have not to be contrasted, nor, since it devolves upon another to tell what he has done, in that form of poetry in which if a man be great, he is also lyrist and might have written an epic, would there seem call to speak of him as poet, otherwise than in reference to how far as such he was artist; but the degree in which one might be poet without being

---

[1] The poet, is one "Who with a man is equal, be he any won- "drous thing 'twixt ape and Plato," is dower'd with the scorn of "scorn, the hate of hate and love of love," is "as a nerve o'er "which do creep the else-unfelt oppressions of this earth," to whom "*nihil humani alienum est,*" and "*a man's a man for a'* "*that.*"

artist is zero,—poetic artist defines poet[1],—and of Browning as artist of any other sort what ground of impression?

As fitting as it is in most cases to confer on a literary man, having effectively presented various subject-matters, designations of which the word artist forms part, *e. g.*, psychological artist, historical, philosophical and the like, yet some scruple would seem in place in case of his having adopted verse as his sole means of expression ; and let Browning have brought home to us truths of as various orders, as much soul-lore, recondite history, and ultimate philosophy, as he may, still 95,000 lines of verse and no prose to speak of, forbid our looking upon him as artist if we may not as poet.

No form of expression is too choice for veritable philosophy, but verse is proper only to one whom perception of the harmony that is and shall be compels to its use, who in spite of all the appearance to the contrary, sees reason for singing, sees even that in the midst of death we are in life and that romance is real.[2]

It founds no claim to the exercise of art, in some moment of release from limitation, to produce a genuine poem, develop a melody or harmony, or have grow under the hand some ideal shape. These things are for comfort to souls grieving over inability to produce any fair or wonderous thing, as testifying to the equal potentiality in us all, but art is far from these happenings and more than merely well-directed effort.

If, now, writing verse more than half a century, of sound mind in sound body, in not the straitest circumstances, all galleries of art, libraries and circles of society open to him, with a

---

[1] "*Mediocribus* (not artists) *esse poetis....non concessere* " *columnae*."

[2] " Does but speak because he must," sings "as linnets sing " hymns unbidden, " Till the world is wrought to sympathy with " hopes and fears it heedeth not."

"lyric love, half angel and half bird," for wife[1], there lay before us simply a few good poems and any number of merely moderate merit, there would be little to say of Browning as poetic artist.

But how different the real state of the case! Even to the twenty-year-old boy, having covertly laid his first gift on the altar he lived to pile so high, came the confirmation of his call in these words of grave seers inspired of Melpomene and Euterpe: —" Whoever he is, he sees the way, is strong, and will arrive." He did see the way, saw it "as birds their trackless way," and has arrived.

Dante Rosetti noted at once in *Pauline* the accents of a brother's voice. It gave that keen critic Fox "the thrill that never failed him as the test of genius." "We felt certain of "Tennyson; we are not less certain of the author of *Pauline*."

John Foster, unaware whether it was the work of youth or age, on reading *Paracelus*, unhesitatingly ranked its author with Shelley, Coleridge and Wordsworth, and, in *Strafford* found only the inherent nobleness of the Lion of England, overshadowing to the poet's view what principle made him its last hope and stronghold; but found therein no note failing of the music answering to this kindlier regard of the man potential rather than actual. Lang finds Browning in " Heap cassia, sandal-buds," in *Paracelsus*, in the central current of lyric verse where Shelley was, elsewhere often in its shallows, but no counsel from its edge, only from on high, could avail one borne upon that tide. Next after *Strafford* came *Sordello* " the obscure and rugged," a poem even fluent in style save for an eddy here and there, and as to its thought, identical with that of a school of men than whom none write plainer prose. Swinburne says, to charge the illuminate who wrote it with obscurity is about as accurate as to call Lynceus purblind.

---

[1] Yet Prov. 11, 10, and " *Wer nie sein Brot....*"

The causes, almost too obvious to state, of anything seemingly peculiar in his expression, are, that he would not resign the ancient rights and uses of poets, revived words of strong sense and clear English ring, used the ellipses natural to impassioned thought, employed the word-order of the English language, not that of the present colloquial only, thereby infusing something of mood and relation into forms that, taken by themselves, no man may say whether they be roots, or stems, or what.

Are they who wield the instrument of thought best, to have no part in moulding it? Is our tongue to know no check to the tendency to which the philologist Sayce says it owes its wide extension, and fall into that state whence result " intellectual " torpor and mental confusion " even **to** Celestials unread in their classics?

And to what end? That we may boast it universal, the medium of commerce[1], of spreading our ideas[2] amongst peoples the rudiments of whose thought we have yet to learn!

"If the red slayer think he slays, or if the slain think he is " slain, they know not well the ways I keep, and pass, and turn " again."—*Bhagavad-Gita.*

" Whence this great creation?....perchance even he knows " not."—[3] *Rig-Veda.*

---

[1] " And honor sinks where commerce long prevails."

" Hang up philosophy, " sink commerce, " hence pageant His- " tory! What care? Juliet leaning amid her window-flowers " ....Doth more avail than these," if they must lose us the ideal.

[2] "Nought but the wide-world story how the earth and " heavens began, how the gods are glad and angry, and a " deity once was man."

[3] *Nullam rem nilo gigni divinitus unquam.*" cf. Milton.

"And one to me are shame and fame."

"Take[1] not this world in hand to make it to your mind.   He "that makes, mars.   Where are many prohibitive enactments, the " people are poor, where many laws and restrictions, thieves mul- "tiply, where legions are quartered, thorns and briars grow." Lao-tse, of whom Confucius, "I know many things,[2] .... how " birds can fly and may be shot, but I have seen the Dragon this " day and how he mounts I cannot tell."   It has been said that Browning combats the philosophy of the time.   Strange if by the word be meant the staple from pulpit and rostrum, the most unphilosophic, unpoetic, inartistic medley, ever honored with the name.

What its burden?   The upholder of the universe needs help: shoulders to the wheel, make the earth a dead level.   For princi- ples and method, read the great gospels of absolute ethics, for motive, appeal to the feelings, and to the power in man to be a devil that he make himself a martyr for the general good.

" Take but degree away, untune that string, and, hark what " discord follows."

On the one hand it's hurrah for freedom, idleness,[3] and drink, on the other, for regulation on regulation, for Puritanic joys, so- cial equality, leisure,[4] vegetables and water.   No need of game laws then, of physicians or vivisection.

---

[1] " Pain thee not each crooked to redress, in trust of her that "turneth like a ball.   Great rest standeth in little business, be- " ware also to spurn an nalle.   Strive not as doth a crook with "a wall.   Daunt thyself that dauntest others' deed, and truth "shall thee deliver, 'tis no dread."

[2] *Inter alia.*   "What you do not like when done to yourself, "do not to others.   Reciprocity is the rule for all one's life." "Limit your wishes to the attainable."

[3] " The very fiends weave ropes of sand
      " Rather than taste pure hell in idleness."

[4] For what?   Every parent of many children knows that few are called to other than the low life of· the most, that two or more must fall that one may stand.

How the crops will ripen in the sun, how amiably, for a few short hours each day, men will contend in the busy mart, and how the strain on one's sympathies will relax, when government takes land and trade in hand and through her hosts of good and faithful servants looks after every red man and white with a tender parent's care!

We shall need no poets then but, in our joy, break forth one and all in some hymn revised.

Whence danger to family, state, church, the many-sided development of mankind, the sphere of personal liberty,[1] whence encouragement to the dreams of anarchy?

From those who would set the world aright, naturally sound in head and heart, but filled with intentions that pave "the "down below," unbalanced by the over-altruism that is but self-regard of irritated nerve, till the voices of the past and present,[2] the refutation of their conclusions by their own premises and the lessons of history, alas, are of no account to them. Whence the nullity of the influence on affairs of the so-called cultured class, well-meaning as it is, and backed by religion, wealth and position? No need to answer, politicians, business men, and common voters all know. Whence sympathy's own undoing, its curdling into the feeling of the keeper of swine for his herd, mingling of attachment, disgust, and the vexation of disappointed individual view and will, that finds but natural expression in blue law, harangue, raca, fool, and even the armed hand? Moral

---

[1] Whose varying wall to keep, justice, that clearest thing, strives with all her might, even mother nature not letting the atoms crowd. See W. von Humboldt.

[2] Yes, of men living, to whom, in a way, we owe food, warmth, and light and medicine and most of the little now known of the forces and laws internal and external to which we must adjust ourselves or die individually and as a people. "That the many "thrive, let them regard the few." Homer, Machiavelli, et al.

contempt[1] of those its function is to make us serve, be served by, and the more enjoy, blindness to the simplest criterion of discrimination between what we know, and knowing not, yet feel sure of, want of trust in Him who holds the helm, to wait for the slow sure march of opinion, scientific and public, to the truth that gives all needed power for good.[2]

What is requisite to the appreciation of *Sordello*, but some preliminary charging of the memory with its main drift and measure,—for that unconscious energy to work upon that is ever helping us to solve our problems, yet which can do nothing with the mind a *tabula rasa*,—the attainment of something like the poet's knowledge of its historical setting, and the intellectual effort inevitable for us in acquiring conceptions that, through this life,

---

[1] " Who feels contempt for any living thing....
" Thought with him is in its infancy."

[2] " Did he drivel," who never turned his back on life or death, let " whatever is, teach, " that the way to remove abuses is " to know how "—not guess or force a guess on any man—" to " stand by the truth attained," and strive from dawn through noonday and "across the sunset colored waters" to catch the gleams of a more rational horizon ; that it is best to keep the whole man sound, every fibre of heart and brain ; that life symmetrical, worth living long, comes of naturalness and degree, placidity and peace of mind won by no infraction on the spheres of others, of humility and trust—without which " the pillared " firmament were rottenness "—: yet no balking of every impulse, rousing of body and soul to mutual enmity, no balancing of abstract right and wrong, till the tide has ebbed—" Where's " abstract Right for me ? " " Youth once gone is gone ; deeds " let escape are never to be done "—no such intentness on saving of the soul as to make it miss life's every goal, no conjectural duty-doing at no matter whose expense : " Held we fall to rise, " are baffled to fight better. Sleep to wake." Did he drivel ?

" There is an evil wrought by want of thought "—
" As well as want of heart."

would have remained far from us if left to our own creative imaginations, unaided, to develop?

Where has more been said, by the timely interchange of sound and silence, rise and fall of voice, and reckoning on no more developed susceptibility to what can thus be conveyed than comes of having heard such men as Raymond, Thaxter, and the like, who follow poets as talent, genius? Without their aid, there is doubt whether we should sense Shakespeare even to the limited extent that we do.

"'Tis but a brother's speech
"We need, speech where an accent's change gives each the "other soul."

It were well to learn before pronouncing anything of Browning's sound without sense, or neither sound nor sense, to whom we owe it. To one who as master of the metres of tongues that are dead, and of many living that were like to have become jargons, by this, but for such as he. One by whom few thoughts embodied in literature or notions of science had not been assimilated, and who making mock of no living or inanimate thing, least of all essayed the bewilderment of any man, whom his every familiar asserts both tried and true, "a poet and a saint," "the hard and rarest union that can be, next Godhead and "humanity."

Of his 313 issues between *Sordello* and the *Ring and the Book*, it seems superfluous to do more than recall to this audience, that they include 7 dramas, averaging over 1600 lines each, sustained hardly without a break, in the form of verse most difficult to sustain; that of one of them Dickens said he would have rather have written it than any work of modern times, and believed from his soul there was no man living (and not many dead) who could have produced it; that of the remaining 307, in no more than 40 has any widely-known critic found any lack of poetic fancy or felicity in its utterance.

" In the *Ring and the Book* and to a great extent in all Brown-
" ing's writings we find what we have been accustomed to find
" in the pages of Shakespeare only."[1]

The musicians among you, at the first hearing of many a master-
piece of classical music, did not know whether you were pleased
or not, and it was only after repeated hearing and much unconscious cerebration following thereon, and perhaps not a few
efforts at reproduction, that its unity of design so broke upon
you that you saw the necessity to it of its every part.

Conceive that between productions such as the *Ring and the
Book* and poems like a *Lover's Quarrel, One Way of Love,* and
In a Gondola, there is such relation as between the *9th Sym-
phony* of Beethoven, and his simple yet rare sweet melodies, and
that not otherwise than as you attain to the appreciation of the
music can you rise to that of the poem.

It is the musician's part to show in what poetry other than
Browning's the effects of his proper art are more wonderfully
reproduced.

Of *Prince Hohenstiel Schwangau, Fifine at the Fair, Red
Cotton Nightcap Country, Pacchiarotto, Jocoseria,* another
time.

"The shaft that slew can slay not one of all the works
" we knew, nor death discrown that many-laurelled head."[2]

Of the *Inn Album* it has been said by one who knows English
poetry, "It will be in men's mouths, when its detractors' ashes
" lie in the dust, and their opinions, if unearthed by any painful
" antiquary, looked at with wonder and contempt."

La Sasiaz, the *Two Poets of Crosic, Dramatic Idyls,* and
Ferishta's Fancies, have done more than interest us all.

Parleyings with Certain People is rich in examples of pure
poetic diction, and would have a grand result could its eulogy of

---

[1] Robert Buchanan.
[2] Swinburne.

Bernard de Mandeville lead any large number of us to look into the pages of the old self-knower and see what manner of men and women we are.

As to renderings from the Greek. None is pronounced more perfect than our artist's of the Alkestis. Prof. Mahaffy considers his hand 'matchless in conveying the deeper spirit of the Greek poets, that he has given a perfectly faithful idea of Herakles, done the odes into adequate metre, and reproduced with *great* art the special Euripidean feature; that his version of the Agamemnon, which John Addington Symonds pronounces "the Herculean achievement of a scholar poet's ripe genius," will probably not permit the rest to retain their well-earned fame; that in *Aristophanes' Apology* he has treated the controversy between Euripides and Aristophanes with more learning and greater ability than all other critics; while Prof. Geddes rejoices that the strongest and subtlest, if not the sweetest poet of the age, was votary at the shrine of the Greek muse.'

No many-lined production of Browning's is obscure or inartistic, but there are lines and passages, discoverable chiefly in the works of his immaturity and those later ones in which he was compelling certain metrical form to new yet fitting service that are both. They have arisen, in the main, from the fact that with him now and then, thought succeeded thought, and fancy, fancy, too rapidly[1] for even his vast speech-resources to furnish forth perfect vesture for them every one. His impulse was ever to fresh effort rather than to return on things done, and thus we have more true poetry and thought from him than had he, like his great contemporary, spent time bringing every line to that perfection his few revisions should satisfy us he could have lent it. Is it his thoughtful *In Memoriam* or his other works that gives Tennyson his hold secure upon our time?

"The strength of poetry is in its thought;....With great ly-"rists, the music is always secondary,....they leave a syllable or

---

[1] "Fast as fancies come: Rudely, the verse being as the mood "it *plaits*." *fancies*

" two rough or even mean..and avoid a perfect rhythm or sweet-
"ness...., lest we lean too definitely on sound,"[1] " Of poetry
" the success is not attained when it lulls and satisfies, but when
"it astonishes and fires us with new endeavor after the unattain-
"able."[2] " The way to miss the first requisite of poetry, organic
"unity, is to give undue attention to parts."[3] What poem of
Browning's lacks it ?

Our subjective hindrance to the understanding of his work is
precisely that to our comprehension of all true science and art,
viz., native and almost ineradicable tendency to the inversion of
the state of every case.   Science exists in refutation of natural
impression, as the hand-maid of art, which, primarily, is the means
of doing what nature has not done for us, as for the rest, of gen-
erating higher perceptions and reconciling the seeming with the
real.   Both have existed since the days of Cain,—whose children
were the first to enter into full possession of the genuine human
estate,—have often changed their habitat, and, to their mutual
prejudice, had their relations inverted in man's esteem.   At the
moment the former is fulfilling its function, in many ways better
than in earlier days, but grown one-sided in method unequal to
the overthrow of certain natural impressions, e. g., that space has
independent existence, that His will is delayed, and abridged in
execution by ours, that there is no trinity, i. e., that the logical
faculty is supreme, and that character is not mere result of breed
and circumstance.[4]

Certainly with these ideas, the evolution of anything must
seem singular, whether of a character by a poet, or of the world
by the ποιητή's. Shakespeare knew us well, that, for the most part,
we should be in the pit, and while blending the representation of
action in character with that of character in action wisely put the
latter in the foreground.   Leading a universal life, omnipresent,
in a way, in others, he had only to contract himself to the dimen-

---

[1] Ruskin.   [2] Emerson.   [3] Horace, in effect.

[4] " *Ein Character bildet sich in dem Strom der Welt.*"

sions of a given individual to be the same for all purposes of representation yet suffered thence no loss of the capacity of his wider self to appreciate the genesis of any character into which he entered.

Göthe and Browning, being feebler imitations of personality, (perhaps only because each an individual, while he may have been more than one), exemplify the process of moving out of self, by expansion, which being our way, if there be any for us, they are more needed by us, who lead no universal life, move not, of ourselves, from out our ruts.

It would be a presumption against the merit of Browning's poetry as a whole, if it did not have to wait awhile for more general acceptance. Dante's waited several centuries; and not a little of Göthe's and some of Shakespeare's till their great spirits had passed away.

Our children are pleased enough to listen to certain of his songs and ballads, the *Cavalier Tunes* are declaimed in the schoolrooms of England with as much animation as anything in ours, showing their power to stir the old loyalty inborn in her youth. We note only 11 in Bryant's collection of 31, and 7 in Dana's of 19 years ago, but large space is given to his poems in the popular English collections of the day.[1] It is safe to say that three of his dramas and 150 of his minor poems prior to his *Men and Women*, are widely read and prized by all people of any degree of feeling and imagination, while those who know the latter and do not care for them are limited in every sense. Only his minor works first won Göthe popular regard, so that, unless as affected by the order of their production, it is as difficult to see anything peculiar in the reception of Browning's work as to find anything exceptional in the amount, the merits, faults, or content thereof.

[2]Are there no obscurities or irregularities in the Greek dramatists or the greatest English, in the latter, no ill-timed playing

---

[1]Whipple puts him next Tennyson, and no other of the century beside them.

[2]Look through Tennyson's work prior to 1850.

with words of double (even simple) entendre, no repetitions or prolixity in him or Homer, no sinking below or rising above the subject in the Latin models?

"Whoever thinks a faultless piece to see, thinks what ne'er was, "nor is, nor e'er shall be." "*Nihil ab omne parte beatum est.*" In Browning you will find no rounded hollow holes, no skin-deep beauty, no shows of a consistency unknown to nature, no cunning of which men say, Lo, behold the art!

By the *Ring and the Book,* he were artist, though he had written his 75,000 lines besides, with the ink that fades in drying. It may not make us competent to a true, but may preserve us from a superficial judgment of poetry, not to be apprehended at sight, to keep in mind the following.

Poetry is not of one order only, yet, of whatever order, must have musical form, and such as is in harmony with the thought and imagery it would convey. The higher sort involves all requisites of the lower and an essential difference therefrom. The excellencies of any example in any species, can, in the nature of the case, rarely be present in like degree. Index of the worth of one is the sum of the degrees in which it fulfils its requisites. The fine arts are of all the most laborious, characterized each by an infinite striving. No one leaps to their heights, which, even to see, requires much clearing of the vision.

Men in general work, constrained by necessity, self-regard, ambition or greed, toward near and oft-attained goals, living, meanwhile, in each other's praise and enjoying not a few of life's good things as they go, but in lieu of these motives, yes, in resistence of the most powerful of them, even of that which leads to lives spent in the service of others "for the peace it gives," what is to sustain the artist's energy directed to a goal that may be reached, never or too late for more than a dying sigh of gladness for having wrought according to the dictates from within?

Who among us so energetic and duty-driven that would not have been appalled at the labor, self-abnegation (as men reckon it), and barrenness of life, often with all its pomp and riches at command, that has lain between great artists and their final triumphs? What of common joy, of joy at all, other than in productive activity in that stretch of 90 years that just enabled Michael Angelo to keep his word and cast the roof of the best known temple to the living God that is built with hands.

But it is to that other aspect of the case, in which the art is laborious, that I would especially direct your attention.

We cannot sense the simplest form of words without a labor of the mind akin in kind though not degree to that of him who utters them. As to origin, every artistic conception is tax on the intellectual imagination of its originator, as to embodiment in sound, or form, or form and color, requires an exercise of physical and psychical powers possible to them only from heredity and long antecedent training, and can look, therefore, only to responsive senses, hearts, and heads, for its comprehension and enjoyment.

While remembering all the pleasing attributes of poetry let us not forget that a example of it, though affording the cleanest cut images, the most charming thoughts, and flowing as smoothly as ever verse flowed, though lacking none of the essentials of the nominal definition of poetry, (any more than man of his, when, as in infancy, he is but a sweet, laughing, land-going biped, before rationality has supervened upon his mere sense-preception, memory and locomotive powers), may yet be destitute of that element by which poetry becomes immortal.

Until it have this, it comes only from the senses and pictorial imagination of its originator, and finds but like resting places in us. " 'Tis greedy of the moment," if pathetic, it but stimulates to self-pity, if gay or sensuous, but favors forgetfulness of interest, if enlivening or martial, confers but short-lived animation or cour-

age, and can be powerful for ill, can fix in memory scenes so revolting as to sicken life, and show so fair the face of matter that many
a spirit has yielded.

It is poetry, but poetry with her feet on the ground, unwinged
before her flight, that has as yet brought nothing down from
heaven, or done anything to lift man thitherward.

Technically, this element in virtue of which any production of
art leaves the level we cling to and beckons us to a higher, is that
its thought shall involve some particularization of the universal;
and pointing to this highest excellence, Aristotle says:

"Poetry is a more philosophic and more serious matter than
"history," being expressive of the universal therein, in short, in
the human, "and should exhibit things as does the painting of
"Zeuxis."

Zeuxis was he who painted for the birds[1] of the air as well as
men, yes, *in æternitatem*, who through contemplation of all the
beauty of woman that the favor of chance, for short, and the
interest of a Grecian state could unveil to him, so far recovered
the archetype of female loveliness to which every woman's
face and shape is more or less conformed that there so glowed
again (with the nameless charm of *das Ewig Weibliche*), in form
and color, the ideal, the daughters of Greece,—under certain circumstances—were wont to dream of, as to make her later poets
sing well-nigh as passionately of the reflex as did the earlier of
the reality. Fully perceptive of this as the one true method in
art, Sir Joshua Reynolds says in substance, "The idea of beauty
"in each species is an invariable one." Would you paint a great
man, paint that consequence in you of having seen him under all
the varying influences incidental to this state of ours, and perhaps somewhat of the impression a life-long intimacy with him
gave his familiars, may be imparted to some of those who view

---

[1] The self-golden-crowned painted alone for the senses, for the
near-sightedness of man. No bird would have pecked his grapes.

your portrait. Would you paint the type of a class, it will be more perfect as it is the more remote from peculiarities. Would you paint man, forget the strength of Hercules in the delicacy of Apollo, etc. "The difficulty of the art of poetry is to exemplify "the universal in the individual."[1] Horace. "The genius of "Browning is to discern in every particular an epitome of cre-"ation, and to set it forth in appropriate form." Milsand.

Here if time served, it would be in order, to lay before you examples of Browning's poetry, some making evident how in the veriest concretes he has brought down to our apprehension the highest ideals, others giving less extraordinary reductions of the many to the one, but all marked by a perfection of poetic rhythm readily perceptible, holding a harmony between sound and sense too striking to escape any one, conveying imagery with a clearness, and infusing stranger-thoughts with a subtlety even more remarkable. But as it is, I must content myself with re-marking that it is to a very different extent and with varying de-grees of directness that great poets exercise their prerogative of showing the individual, exemplification of the all, that the pecu-liarity of *his* greatness who "knew man as he was and might be," resided in his ability to speak to men on all levels, by so represent-ting even the highest universals, that in him sense lies within sense in such wise that any man may read and rest content with that obvious to him, nor be compelled to view any depth beyond, while, as a rule, we must get Browning's bottom thought or none.

---

[1] Not characterization by mere generalization of finite attri-butes into infinite, good or bad, not representation of perfection beyond nature, or complete absence of grace, in man or woman. Here lies the open secret of non-formal excellences of poetry, not merely, *e. g.*, why, from *Tartufe* "*un tartufe, tartuferie,*" why, "armor," in the lines, "Armor and ashes reach the house of "each" is better than "sword," but, quite generally, the reason of the pregnancy of the passages of a poet as compared with the tumidity of a mere writer of smooth verse.

Now what to us, when done, is this triumph of art that such labored expression has been needed to give a notion of? By compelling us to enter into the souls of others, that is, to entertain in earnest the dominant ideas of the characters it represents, it engenders, in spite of us, impulsions to all their actions, good and bad, through their sentiments and volitions become our own, children of those ideas[1], and thus whether they be such as burst the bonds of our narrowness or sink us in the limitations of other of less heart and mind than we chance to have, we are made to learn that we exist not alone in our own place but in *extrariis, extraneis, etiam alienissimis,* and so that we, as individuals, Mr. or Mrs., so and so, are each but a sum, a particular collection of impressions, sentiments and impulses seated for a time in a sentient thinking centre that shall more and more rid itself of them. And what is this but our universalization, clue to mutual understanding, first step to perception of an inner and common nature without which were no outer and lower?

The perfect agreement between the deeper content of the poetry of Homer and Æschylus, Chaucer, Shakespeare and Göthe with what of truth we deem ourselves in possession of through other instrumentalities than poetic insight, and the healthful influence it spreads all round by begetting even in those who cannot grasp principial thoughts, the sentiments bred of them,

---

[1] "There is nothing but *thinking* makes it so." 'Thought is the "root of all," and everywhere, when the days are fulfilled, breeds feeling and desire, but, according to soil. Only in concrete unity with its natural results in a soul alert and not overfull of error, or in some rank rich garden of nature, does it other itself in poetry. Hence merely knowing something of versification and the thought as such of a poem does not enable one to tell whether its form is consonant with its content; to this is necessary the frame of mind of the author, for in that frame or mood lies unified the thought, sentiment, and longing, whence flows the verse:

"Great poets are to be judged by the frame of mind they induce."—*Emerson.*

confirms its worth, while the affluence of Browning's thought and its identity with theirs, of itself, includes him in their ranks, for though each was original, himself alone in the handling of his matter, his thought was not peculiar to himself, rising from same fountain head only with murmur and in measure different, and in whom that thought dwells in all its fulness, as in them, not the laborious inkling thereof that is in us, it begets its poetic body, all the imagery and music that can shadow it forth. Its impulse to poetic rhythm affects even the utterances of the prosaic men it reaches, but, owing to their imperfect tuning, results in so ill-regulated recurrence of what we expect, that while we value their insights we deem the style hybrid, amendable only by much reference to the prose of poets. Is the thought[1] of the Greek poets revived for us in the greatest English and German, too high for the many to gather, their sentiments such as only the elect can share, the beauty they beheld too rare for common perceptions, then turn the gospel back into Latin, for the loudest notes in all the poesy of both are but preludes or echoes of the words thereof, falling like strokes of an axe on the roots of the Upas-tree of human error.

As Browning has been called this and that, so, with the same ineptitude, has his poetry been styled metaphysical, religious, ethical, æsthetic, emotive, scientific.

No poetry of the higher sort, and such is his, will bear to be thus named, unless these terms are disburthened of most of their associations, but let them be applied to it, and, perhaps, even from the measure in which they are found to have application thereto,

---

[1] Thought plainer to those who know what life is, what the struggle for bread or sense, and against excess or weakness, yes, to publicans, sinners and idlers, than to the victims of elegant leisure, self-consciousness, moral sense, fastidiousness, and conventionality. Limited the light of those who reject it, limited the sweetness of those who blame at all, and, tried by these tests, limited, very, the number of the cultured.

some notion may accrue to us of what in verity may be metaphysics, religion and ethics.

As to its being metaphysical.

It says to those who curl the lip at the notion of a science of the self-evident, that there are no metaphysics of the sort they figure save in their all too common sense; to those preferring, to the assurance seated in the head as hope in the heart,—in accord with the eternal fitness of things for this excursus from the state it no longer enters into us to conceive—, the subjective certainty that comes of repetition and assumptions of which no proof is possible, that, but for her hints, their mathematics were still in the Euclidean stage, their astronomy Ptolemaic, and their chemistry, alchemy, their theory meagre as to thought, things, word and deed, and the wonders of their working few[1]: to those who seek the soul's abode, that it resides in no subject for their dissection, in no pineal gland, or corpus callosum;[2] to those who, setting forth with condescending comment the philosophy of "the father of "those that know," inculcate the empty notion of a world all by itself out there, of which an image is wrought somehow in and by us, that, so far from merest glimpse of an original which might in conscience entitle them to call what we behold an image, there

---

[1] "Science must plainly attain its highest development in the "work of a future poet." Maudsley. cf. *Das Märchen Göthe's.*

[2] Knowest thou not what thou deemest thy abode hath its abode in thee, not indeed as figment of thy dream is of thy substance built, and on thy state of revery, sleep or madness doth depend, but for thy tenement to seem to many another soul with thee, till this its function fail and its element form afresh, a figment of thy maker's dream, that maketh all the world for thee, is thy abode, none thou, for thou in him dost live and move and have thy being, and wouldst thou share that glorious dream, then must thou wear each mortal coil with which His fancy thee indue, as blind-worm squirm or eagle fly, as lion roar or man implore. o. h., *i. e., oratio commodi causâ hibrida.*

is no exterior to consciousness, that they take the real for reflex
of its shadow, that the soul is circumference of the universe,
that neither darkness nor silence lies beyond its limits, that the
mind is its own place, occupying not, yet filled, that the great
potter moulds no clay but soul, that there is no stuff but that
which dreams are made of, the stuff we are.[1]

"Offend not the soul which is its own refuge and witness." It
has to say to those who initiate their bent, owe their moral excel-

---

[1] Anæsthetized by the fumes of many laboratories, we calmly
hear how the 18th century established the indestructibility of
matter, the 19th that of energy, and that perhaps the next may
do as much for soul, and then go dream that it, the source
whence the centuries unroll, perchance may die upon the ether
waves,—O Parmenides, in this dire need of ours, speak, but
through some glory of our age lest we hear not—; narcotized by
the smoke of our own unacceptableness, we bow the knee to
"the fighter for Israel, whose portion is his people, for whom
"alone he lets the rain fall," and rise to treat with contempt
his chosen, whose notions—useful, accurate inversions of invisible things, to see them by, now clear to them—born of the
splendid imagination of the egoism unfathomable of their prime,
are the common borrowed furniture of our barren minds.—
"He spares the world only for Christians' sake." O Luther,
great reformer!—exalted with supposititious regard for the laws
of thought, and fascinated with an imaginary deliverance of
consciousness, the legitimate inference from which would be as
surely hell as heaven, we smile the smile of superior intellectu-
ality and moral dignity at the propositions "A is non-A " and
"man's God is his higher self," and knowing that fire burns,
the many ways to physical distress and death, that to violate the
sympathetic principle—, part and parcel of us, as truly as is sensi-
tiveness to heat and cold—, is the way to a remorse or shame
shrieking for the night that shuts the eye in death annihilative,
we conclude that, *sine arbitrio*, we shouldn't be responsible and,
unrestrained by freedom, might do as we please.

lence just a little to themselves, for whom the truth is not quite
compulsory,—" No more than the passive clay disputes the potter's
" act, can the whelmed mind disobey Knowledge the cataract"
—who are not utterly at the mercy of it and love, on whose
principle, nature made monster and the brother potential devil,
e'en charity for God is *vox et praeterea nihil*, that could their even
more than metaphysical imagination of fundamental caprice[1] be
replaced in us by any vision of Him who loves because he must,
the clash of part with part and part with whole would end,[2]
that all motive, all might, the world of longing at the bottom of the realized, the one force of science, the omnipotence

---

[1] "*Arbitrium dei asylum ignorantiae est.*"   " He saw through
" his own soul the marvel of the everlasting will."—cf. *Sordello.*
A father holds his sleeping son in arms and wonders at his
face ; could that useful thing " whence death and all our woe,"
usurp that father's heart, the child would wake in dread, and
drifted out of child's estate, with him, precocious, cower before
imagined chance.   o. h. When the true interest of a nature is as
obvious to it as it can be and it goes against the same, the more
intense its selfishness, the greater its impotence to follow its
own dictate.   And the youth Elihu, of the kindred of the ele
vated said unto the dreamer of judgments alone for the wicked
and unrepentant, to the judge according to works, and to the de-
claimer of the portion of the wicked, I have waited for your
words, days should speak and multiplied years teach, yet great
men are not ever all wise, nor the aged in possession of all wisdom.   I may not flatter lest I vanish, nor with your speech am I
to speak to the afflicted.   O, Job, though thy flesh be consumed,
and soul abhor the meat of desire, and bones stick out, yet if
there be a messenger with one to show unto man his upright-
ness, his flesh shall be fresher than a child's and he shall see his
face with joy.   And they went, the trio, to beg the prayers of
him who should live again, Elihu, unto the business whereunto
he was called. cf. Rom. ix. 18 and 29 ; 1 Cor. x. 29.

[2] cf. Göthe.

of theology, are subject to Reason, rational necessity, the law of love and laws, the fate of Æschylus, the first mover of Aristotle, the logos of St. John.

"One and all of Ate held in thrall," [1] "Ate, power mislead-"ing all."[2]

"Over gods sits law supreme. The gods are under Law,—so "do we judge,—and therefore can we live, While right and "wrong stand (to our feeling) separate forever." [3] "Did not "an appointed fate constrain the fate from gods."[1] "When to "destruction He will plague a house, He plants among its "members guilt and sin."[1]

"Destiny that hath this lower world to instrument and all "that is in it." [4] "O, Thou eternal Mover." [4]

"All's love and all's law," "springing from the realm of the "indwelling only God."[5]

And it has further to say to these same, lay no blame anywhere, lest your wasted inner sense define for you no vaguest outline of that connection, referred to in Eph. iv. 5, John xv. 5.

"In whom is life forever more, and whom existence in its "lowest forms includes."

"All things unto our flesh are kind in their descent and being; "to our mind in their ascent and cause."[6]

"In the beginning was self alone[7], the self in all ourselves, to "be grasped only by him who he himself grasps," exclusive in its self-regard, for there was naught beside, one and one-minded,

---

[1] Æschylus. [2] Homer. [3] Euripides. [4] Shakspere. [5] Sophocles.

[6] "Life is not a contrast to non-living matter but a further "development of it." — *Maudsley.*

[7] "Friendless was the mighty Lord of all and felt defect."

now many and many-minded, yet still it is as though a pact[1], bound us each to each, or, nerve[2] with more than the pneumogastric's power to pain, ignored, else turning policy to pleasure.

Remorse is sympathy struggling to be free, a thorn that groweth in and in till it shall pierce the heart, till I shall cease to think of me and give my thought entire to thee, O, brother wounded whether by hand of mine or thine or any other, which the need that evil come, hath served, o. h.

Some nerves are ever tense, those binding us to kindred, our choices and our issue, but as little to be severed are our connections with the millions in our land, and yet they're few to those that bind us to the many of mankind. Affection must lose itself

---

[1] "From endless time their ears have rung with words by angel "voices sung, Art thou not bound to God? they cried, and the "blest, Yes! whole hosts replied." "The Sofis suppose an express "contract on the day of eternity without beginning between "created spirits and supreme soul from which they were de-"tached."—*Sir W. Jones.*

[2] Look to that nerve for "the something not 'outer' self that "works for righteousness, for the element whereby selfishness is self-corrective, for all there is of any "worm that dieth not," or of any moral dynamic calculated to imple us along ways that might augment human happiness, but are missed, by most, from disregard of those who have revealed them—, Lao-tse, Buddha, Aristotle, Christ, Paul, Mohammed, Choo-tse, Hegel, Lotze, Huxley, Spencer, Browning, and the like, each in his degree. In the depth where all is wanting save the pain that one can feel, a rope is coiled about me, and looking on its fibres I can see heartstrings. . all twisted up for me, o. h. cf. *Eugene Sue.* "I know not where "His islands lift their fronded palms in air, I only know I cannot "drift beyond His love and care.'"

in patriotism as that in universalism, and of these three, the first and last are purest.[1]

"For I dipped into the future, far as human eye could see.
" Saw the vision of the world, and all the wonder that would be.
" . . . . Till the war drums throbbed no longer, and the battle flags
" were furled in the Parliament of man, and the federation of the
" world. There the common sense of most shall hold a fretful
" realm in awe, and the kindly earth shall slumber, lapt in universal law."

Now for the applicability of the rest of these poetic epi-
thets to this poesy. Religious in the ordinary sense! What
great poet has not fallen from Olympus who tried to make it so?

---

[1] " I dream of a day when an English statesman shall arise
with a heart too large for England, having courage in the face of
his countrymen to assert of some suggested policy, " This is good
" for your trade, is necessary for your domination ; but it will
" vex a people hard by, it will hurt a people further off, it will
" profit nothing to the general humanity ; therefore away with
" it."—*Mrs. Browning.* " What greed has grasped, many folk
" has caused to live forlorn." " *Dulce et decorum* . . . .," yet even
that last of those true old Romans, who acted straight up to their
light, to what was duty for them, and did not go beyond it into
any speculative, saw e'er his eyes closed that the principles of
murdered Cæsar must prevail, and that they were wider, though
not yet the widest. " C. In such a time as this it is not meet
" that every nice offence should bear a comment. Many have
" wished noble Brutus had immortal Cæsar's eyes.—B. He
" would be crowned. How that might change his nature? He
" may, then lest he may, prevent. I have not known when his
" affection swayed his reason. O, Julius Cæsar, thy spirit walks
" abroad and turns our swords into our proper entrails."

"Religion makes a rhapsody of words" not poetry.[1]

Religious? That lays again the injunction to raise no tearful eye, no pathetic voice to the invisible—no respecter of persons,

---

[1] Poetry proceeding from unimpaired intellectual imagination and love of nature and man has for content the universal in all religions, views, feelings and longings of men, and is characterized by the massive common sense of Shakespeare, the optimism of Sophocles, Göthe, and Browning, and the humanity of Euripides, Terence, Lucretius, Horace, and Shelley. The imagination of genius generous to the traditional gives birth to the spectacularism of Dante's *Inferno;* dwelling on notions of superior beings and Hebraic judgments, to that of Milton's epic, the former reflecting the dark accidental side, both of Eastern and Western catholicism, the latter the like side of our protestantism; occupied with the perfect and the moral, yet kept in vigor by exceptional rapport with nature, to Wordsworthian heat-lightnings on expanses of vacuity; entangled in the skirts of philosophy, to Coleridgian Eng-Ger, or dream flow of words in fancy's train. But what outcome from both Dante and Milton, when genius threw off its trammels! Especially from the former as the more universal, conformed, and attached to the real. Tradition is conservatrix of natural impressions, especially of such as are flattering to our native egoism, (*e. g.,* that there is blame somewhere) and the necessary though not so aggreeable corollaries. What so obvious as that the religion of us (325,000,000, white, red and black), is retaining its hold on this bescienced age, only by eclipsing its bad text with its good or by borrowings..... 2 Thes. i. 9, by Rom. xi. 24 and 26, "My law is law of grace for all"?—Islamism with her singular aptitude for the rational, when at low ebb elsewhere, began the process long ago, and there is hope, if he hold them not at full arm's length that 370,000,000 yellow and brown men may, to their gain, return our compliments in kind, and even well-based Brahmanism yield a point or two—let young widows' hair grow and possibly some day even let them speak, unshorn, and uncovered, in the temple.

heeding us no more nor less than the little sparrows that fall, shaping the ends of us both alike—, till all the seen is loved and reverenced, "above, around and under." "In all line and "authentic place," and "self itself," as unit midst the rest—; that teaches there is no consciousness of the infinite, only of the infinity of our own. He that hath seen me hath seen the principle[1] of his being, yet I am but its immanency in you, and

"Naught availeth but a new creature," the extinction of us by the higher self, "το κεινοῦν ὡς ἐρώμενον."

"Thee our hearts yearn after as a bride that glances past us "veiled, but ever so that none the veil from what it hides may "know. Thee throughout the universe, wherein thou dost thy-"self reflect and through eyes of him whom man thou madest, "scrutinize."

"The individual soul works through the shows of sense up to "an outer soul as individual too—to find at length, God, man, or "both together mixed." "What can be known of God is mani-"fest;" that inculcates no *contemptum mundi*, but that life is its own reward.

"'Tis life of which our nerves are scant, more life and fuller "that we want." "Ends accomplished turn to means." "Mere "living! how fit to employ all the heart, and the soul and the "senses forever in joy." "*Dux vitae, dia voluptas....At non* "....*bene sine puro pectore vivi.*"

Ethical! That knows no non-Aristotelian virtue, "Take but de-"gree away[2],"—delivers no moral verdict, beholds no falls into the

---

[1] Whole wholly in each of its parts, but exhausted by none. seen of you only in the measure in which I unveil in you the rationality, beauty, and sympathy, unlimited, hidden in the invisible. "To know is opening out a way for the imprisoned "splendor to escape," no entry-way "for light supposed to be without."

[2] "They say best men are moulded out of faults and, for the "most, become much more the better for being a little bad."

gulf in the little slips[1] of men and women, teaches *qui vitia odit homines odit*[2], that conscience is but fear, fear of the rise of sympathy in us with the power of remorse—, "conscience doth "make cowards of us all"—, sees heroism in crime, exacts as much admiration for greatness of soul when exhibited by the so-called bad as by the good. "Man the actual! Nay, praise the potential,"— that affords us naught to quote in favor of our pet reforms, shows that only through passion can passion be refined[3], and recognizes as the bottom and enduring requirement of our nature, a dramatic existance and no saints' rest.

Æsthetic! That can see beauty in ugliness, good in evil, truth in error, hope in ill-success, hides no blood-red thread in the warp and woof of life, yet seeing no sin, no perfect martyrs or horrors of wickedness, easily avoids all extremes, makes beauty's measure a side not so simple[4], that must be touched before it dawns upon us in things or actions, before either the golden section or the golden

---

[1] "Gently scan your brother man, still gentler sister woman; "though they may go a kennin' wrang, to step aside is human. "One point must still be greatly dark, the moving why they do "it. And just as lamely can ye mark How far perhaps they "rue it." Is. lxv. 5. John viii. 9.

[2] "*De vitiis nostris scalam nobis facimus.*"

[3] "Our loves are portals to higher" forever barred till the lower have been passed. "*Cras amet qui nunquam amavit, quique* "*amavit cras amet.*"

[4] "No notice of identity without recollection of the blessed-"ness of peace, no seeing contrast without glimpse sometimes of "the hatefulness of enmity, sometimes enjoyment from mutual "completion of opposites, no discernment of symmetry or equi-"poise, without stirring of the pain and pleasure of secure repose, "of bondage under laws. The world becomes alive to us through "power to see in forms the joy and sorrow of existence they "hide."—*Lotze.*

"*Aller Genuss besteht in Befreiung von Noth oder Pein.*"

mean wear it for us, that it is for every sake, with reference beyond itself, addressed not to sentimentality, (the subjective feeling and judgment of utility of these and those) but to the co-sentiment of men and whole being of each. " Fast by the threshold of Jove's[1] "court are placed two casks, one stored with evil, one with good." " I make peace and create evil."

Ye are subject to vanity not willingly, but in hope, and by reason of him who doeth all things well, and worketh in you not only to do but to will, and though evil must come and woe to him by whom it cometh, yet no woe is worthy to be taken into account with the glory that shall be revealed in you as the ages roll on.[3] " Else I avert my face, nor follow into that dim sequestered state where God unmakes but to re-make the soul he else made first in vain."[2]

" Evil belongs as necessarily to the whole as that the torrid "zone must burn and Lapland freeze, that there be a temperate "region." " Where the salt marshes stagnate, crystals branch ; "Blood dries to crimson ; Evil is beautified in every shape. " Thrust beauty then aside and banish Evil? Wherefore ! After "all, is Evil a result less natural than good." " Crime involves "the penalty and all atone." " The members of God war to- "gether, (by the sacrifice of the innocent and just, the world goes "on), yet in the sphere of this all, love is power and hate is im-

---

[1] " Next Him Pallas," beauty complete, fountain of all knowl- edge, wisdom, and art, blending of harmony and discord, control- ler of Ares, reprobation on her shield and mercy behind, Minerva *operosa, mens cui regnum Totius tributum est,* Neith, of veil unlifted because none may know from the identity of contradic- tories it hides, that mystic ever-worn garment of the All. " Our "life is nature's garment and her shroud." " *So schaff*" *ich am sausenden Webstuhl der Zeit, und wirke der Gottheit lebendiges Kleid.*"

[2] " Only through knowledge of evil, comes man to knowledge "of right, only in struggle with blindness, through aeons, his "sight."—*E. A. Conner.*

[3] *J. N. J.*

"potence." "None of mortal race shall know a course un-
"marked by woe." Yet "courage, my child! In heaven He is
"....commit thy bitter griefs to him and forget not nor be
"angry with thine enemies." "Confusion to thy sight moves
"regular; the unlovely scene is bright. Thy hand, educing good
"from evil brings to one apt harmony the strife of things. One
"ever-during law still binds the whole....But when....wide
"from life's chief good they headlong stray....Father, disperse
"these shadows of the mind from thy off-spring, image, and echo,
"of thy eternal word."

"The truth shall make you free."[1]

"Both the holy forms are one, and what as Beauty here is won,
"we shall as Truth in some hereafter know."

Emotive?[2] That would rid us of all passions, acquaint with
the composure of the wider view, beget the calm of beauty's
spell, inspire the tranquility of the love that casteth out fear, and
still the revolt of pity by teaching that fate is kind.[3]

---

[1] "*Wendet zur Klarheit Euch liebende Flammen die sich
"verdammen, heile die Wahrheit; dasz sie vom Bösen froh sich
"erlösen, um in dem Allverein selig zu sein.*"

[2] "Of those things only should one be afraid, which have the
"power of doing others harm, of the rest, no."—*Dante.*

[3] Tragedy is to remind us that all things happen according to
nature, comedy to cure of insolence, contempt and disgust. "If
"thou art delighted with what is shown on the scenic stage, thou
"shouldest not be troubled with what takes place on the real. To
"the integrity of the all, himself included, is necessary what is
"brought on any man, happening him from the most ancient
"causes spun with his destiny," cf. Arist. and M. Aurel. "What
"is not good for the hive is not good for the bee." "Me
"and my children, if the gods neglect, this has its reason too."
"Ripneus fell too, than whom, a juster, truer man was not in
"Troy. But the gods judged not so." "There is no great and
"small for the soul that maketh all," neither is it increased nor
diminished, and its *interest* in the spectacle of life is at the highest, when it is most wretched.

"Dry up your tears, and stick your rosemary on this fair corse."

"O the cry did break against my very heart."

"Be collected, no amazement, tell your piteous heart there's "no harm done."

"Till unseemly debate turn concord—despair, acquiescence in fate."

Scientific? That lays a leaf in the dead love's hand all un-witting that her soul was but a transient phenomenon incidental to the play of the universal energy, that says the "human time "shall 'never' close its eyelids 'nor' the human sky be gathered "like a scroll." "*Nil desperandum.*" "*Alia origo nos expec-*"*tat, alium rerum status,*" "when the soul shall fall from out "this envelope." "I know there shall dawn a day—is it here "on the homely earth? Is it yonder worlds away, where the "strange and new have birth.... Some where, below, above, shall "a day dawn—this I know—when Power, which vainly strove, "my weakness to o'erthrow shall triumph." "What if earth "be but the shadow of Heaven and things therein, each to the "other like, more than on earth is thought." *Raphael to Adam.* "We strive and thrive,....fare ever there as here." "Ages "past the soul existed, here an age 'tis resting merely, and "fleets again for ages." "And for my soul, what can it do to " that? "

Pausing for no choice of words, I should call this poetry, emancipating, incentive to action, rational when possible—"it is "better being sane than mad"—but action rather of Byronic naturalness than none. "The native hue of resolution is sick-"lied o'er with the pale cast of thought; and enterprises of "great pith and moment with this regard their currents turn "awry, and lose the name of action." "The flighty purpose "never is o'ertook unless the deed go with it." "Let a man "contend to the uttermost for his life's set prize, be it what it "will." "In the beginning was the deed," "the trinity of "thought, word and deed." "The practic part of life must be "mistress to all this theoric," yet, "whatever praises itself

"but in deed, devours the deed in praise." "Life's no resting
"but a moving, let your life be deed on deed."

The function of art is to help the spirit in its return from
otherness to itself, and science but another back-leading way to
that estate in which no exercise of the discursive intellect was
requisite, and no art that is named or conceivable had any reason
for being, or, if there be no God without creatures and no
creature without God, it is a goal never to be reached, because no
living thing shall rise all-sidedly at once, intellectually, æstheti-
cally and sympathetically, to the height at which the creature-
nature would cease.

"Many the wanderings of the soul in imaginations, opinions,
"and led by the logical faculty, but the life of reason, the alone
"inerratic, is the mystic port to which Homer conducts Ulysses
"after abundant wanderings." Proclus. cf. Dante, Par. iv,
124, 129.

"I may put forth angel-plumage once unmanned but not
"before." ("They that level at my abuses reckon up their own."
"Man's most Godlike, being most a man.") "I have done; and
"if any blame me, thinking that merely to touch in brevity the
"topics I dwell on were unlawful....I refer myself to Thee
"instead of him."

" *Orandum est ut sit mens sana in corpore sano.*"

E. H. MERRELL.

BROWNING'S PHILOSOPHY.

In that European capital which is especially distinguished for its art treasures, one Master pre-eminently, a native of the land, has left his record on its walls. With a firm hand, and in glowing colors, he reproduces the life of his own age; Kings and Queens and courtiers, warriers, artisans, gay revellers, hermits, beggars, saints. It needs but an enchanters wand and the figures of Velasquez would leap from the canvas with human passions, love and hate, cruelty and craft, as they lived, spoke and acted more that two centuries ago. Such a great magician, such a surpassing artist, we invoke when we speak the name of Robert Browning.

In his long list of writings appear a medley of characters, created by the hand of genius; each true to its type, yet of distinct individuality; and each working out its appointed purpose in the author's mind; as he says himself,

> "Love, you saw me gather men and women
> "Live or dead or fashioned by my fancy,
> "Enter each and all and use that service."

Through study of these characters, their "Joys and sorrows, hopes and fears, belief and disbelieving" the disciple of Browning arrives at his philosophy.

Its fundamental principle is generally admitted to be the possibility and grandeur of soul-development—an advancement gained through manifold experience. Divine love and human passion, disappointment, failure, even sin, are important elements.

Growth there must be, if there is life; "Progress, man's distinctive mark alone, not God's and not the beasts;" with growth, even distorted, one-sided ultimately comes expansion; defeat ends in triumph; the soul attains.

(55)

In the three earliest poems this is the grand idea. In *Pauline* the soul-history absorbs the whole monologue. In *Sordello* it runs a thread of thrilling interest through the confused picture of Lombard life in the days of the Troubadors. In *Paracelsus* is portrayed what seems like the decay of the soul—an earnest youth seeking knowledge for its best use ends as a broken down charlatan—and yet through apparent failure comes the awakening to truth. With "God's lamp pressed close to his heart" Paracelsus expires.

Worldly success is never the reward which Browning's romance bestows upon its heroes. The Provencal minstrel, with his last breath trampling on the Imperial badge, the Great Doctor in the mad-house cell, these have another recompense than that of earth. The little silk-winder, whose insignificant existence moves in one day so many of the great world above her, goes back to the factory ignorant of the higher fate to which her birth assigned her. The wonderful influence Pippa works upon such different characters, was as subtle as the electric fluid which quivers in the still atmosphere of a summer night. Nothing illustrates better the soul-philosophy of the great poet than this short drama. No effect of personal contact turns the scale; no social supremacy; no words of wisdom; neither flattery nor sarcasm; but the unrecognized presence of one pure being, guileless and single minded, wrought the change which lifted each actor to a higher stage in the great evolution. So it was, in a still more marked degree with Pompilia, moving in maiden innocence amid corrupting influences in the town, in the Church, in her home. The divine spark in her breast awoke an answering fire in the heart of the frivolous young priest, and through him kindled into enthusiasm Roman lawyers, the ignorant populace, even the cynical worldlings of the Court. The grand old Pope himself felt the celestial flame of that child-like spirit, and spread its radiance in a sublime burst of eloquence.

In *A Blot in the Scutcheon* the interest centers on the rapid development of noble qualities through secret guilt, and in spite of the tragedy we feel that there was a triumph at the end. Although a stern moralist might shrink from such an interpretation there can be no doubt it is what the author intended. In stating Browning's philosophy one must admit that it regards deliberate sin and unrestrained passion as factors in soul regeneration, or at least as stages in soul-advancement. The fascination of psychological analysis leads to the depiction of intricacies and tortuous windings of the human heart and conscience which seem at times like bewildering sophistry.

A grander note is sounded in the exaltation of love, as the true mainspring of action throughout the poems and dramas.

" All the world is beauty, and knowing this is love and love is duty " ;

" Life is just our chance in the prize of loving love " ;

" Since we love we know enough " ; and

" Love bids touch truth, endure truth and embrace truth " ;

" Love preceding power, and with much power always much more love " ;

With the fifty men and women this is the controlling influence and among them many different aspects of love are presented, culminating in the intense devotion and exquisite tenderness of the verses addressed to his wife. In those of later years inspired by her memory is a clear unwavering belief in immortality which lifts into a higher atmosphere the bond uniting them on earth.

It is in relation to the belief in a future life that we meet another tenet of the poet's philosophical creed, namely—the inevitable imperfection and limitation of this existence and the need of waiting for another sphere to complete the development of the soul. This is the key note of *Sordello*, where the plague-spot is " Thrusting in time eternity's concern."

Rabbi Ben Ezra says :—

  " For thence—a paradox

  " Which comforts while it mocks—

  " Shall life succeed in that it seems to fail ? "

And Bishop Blougram :—

> "Not to fancy what were fair in life,
> "Provided it could be,—but finding first
> "What may be, then find how to make it fair—
> "Up to our means, a very different thing."

Most consoling is the idea as expressed in the lines on a group of two mutes :—

> "Only the prism's obstruction shows aright
> "The secret of a sunbeam, breaks its light
> "Into the jewelled bow, from blankest white,
> "So may a glory from defect arise."

And the same thought is distinctly conveyed in *Andrea del Sarto* :—

> "Ah! but a man's reach should exceed his grasp,
> "Or what's a heaven for?"

It is suggested by the difficulty of adjustment to finite life which Lazarus feels in returning to earth, "It should be" balked by "here it cannot be," as the Arab Physician expresses it. This is a lesson which can be profitably learned only in the clear light of that anticipation of a grander and higher life which distinguishes Browning from many writers of the time. Where even Tennyson hesitates he never falters. From his boyhood's verse to the old man's Epilogue rings throughout the clear affirmation of belief in the unending life of the soul, and up to this one point in the recognition of a great First Cause all his philosophy tends.

The burden of social problems which weighs so heavily on thinkers of the present day never disturbs his buoyant optimism. Assuming as he does that this world is but the portal to an endless life he views calmly the incompleteness, the wasted opportunities and thwarted purposes which seem to many of us so preplexing an element in human affairs. To him blighted careers and lives of promise cut short are—

> "On earth the broken arcs, in the heaven a perfect round."

The discordant notes of this planet will be part of the grand harmony of the hereafter. "Even hate is but a mask of love"; there is "Good in evil and hope in ill success."

This grand sweep of outlook, this ardent and radiant belief is characteristic of a poet whose gaze has been rather far up into the heavens than down on the base things of earth. If the image of down-trodden humanity suffering from sore injustice arouses in Browning no indignation, it is perhaps because he especially of all sages in our time has bent his vision starward into infinite space; "Look east where whole new thousands are"; and into eternity, reading there the purposes of the Almighty.

In our day and generation there may be great reformers, eloquent preachers, sweet singers—there will not soon arise another philosopher like Robert Browning. If he never becomes the poet of the people he has left a message to be transmitted to them. It may be one side of the truth to teach that "when pain ends gain ends too," that out of failure comes attainment and out of evil good; that this world must be of one limited opportunity and that "imperfection is perfection hid." But to many darkened souls such a philosophy will be one of enlightenment and a widening of vision towards revelation itself. If those of us who are engaged in a battle with evil cannot reconcile ourselves to its existence, even through the eloquence of poetry, we can fully and freely take heart from the strong words penned at Asolo last September :—

> "At noon-day in the bustle of man's work-time
> "Greet the unseen with a cheer!
> "Bid him forward, breast and back as either should be,
> "Strive and thrive! cry 'Speed, fight on, fare ever
> "'There as here!'"

ARRIA S. HUNTINGTON.

BROWNING AS A DRAMATIST.

Browning is essentially a dramatic poet. He loves to express abstract thoughts in a concrete fashion. He never allegorizes. His characters are always real flesh and blood, and their thoughts are a natural part of them.

Some time ago, I was invited to attend the Browning Club in a great city, renowned for its thought and culture. I heard *The Flight of the Duchess* beautifully read, and afterwards commented upon. One gentleman made a most interesting and poetic speech, in which he set forth that the Duchess was The Soul dissatisfied with its mean surroundings, and aspiring heavenward towards larger Freedom and Light. The Duke was "Prosaic Circumstance," that seeks to chain down the "Aspiring Soul." The Gypsy was "Opportunity" or something of the sort. When he had sat down, the president called upon me for a few remarks; and I found, to my astonishment, that I was looked upon with great reverence in my representative capacity as being at the time president of the oldest Browning Club then existing in the country. He asked me to explain to the younger club the secret of our success and our permanence. I said first, that we had all manner of minds in our club, Catholic, Episcopalian, Presbyterian, Congregationalist, Methodist, Unitarian, Hebrew; that the freest discussion, theological or other, accompanied by the deepest respect for each other's honest thought, was the unwritten law of the club. We had our allegorical minds, too, as well as those prosaic literal minds, whom I myself may represent. We had those who could not only deeply appreciate, as I myself could do, but also cordially agree, to the smallest particular, with the splendid exposition of the gentleman who had just sat down; while the prosaic party, to which I myself

belong, would say, " it is all very beautiful, but the trouble is
" that it is *not* Browning." The Duchess is not " The Soul," but a
very lovely young person, who at last becomes wearied to death
with the Duke, who is not " Prosaic Circumstance," but an exceedingly prosaic, pedantic and over-bearing individual : while
the Gypsy is just a gypsy and that is all, who to the day of her
death will be filled with the wild desire for the free life of hill
and dale, which all wild creatures feel. It is for just this
life that the young Duchess pants.

We had a grand battle over the splendid invocation to " Lyric
" Love " in *The Ring and the Book.*

" O Lyric Love, half-angel and half-bird
" And all a wonder and a wild desire,—
" Boldest of hearts that ever braved the sun,
" Took sanctuary within the holier blue,
" And sang a kindred soul out of his face,—
" Yet human at the red-ripe of the heart,—
" When the first summons from the darkling earth
" Reached thee amid thy chambers, blanched their blue,
" And bared them of the glory—to drop down,
" To toil for man, to suffer or to die,—
" This is the same voice : can thy soul know change ?
" Hail then, and harken from the realms of help !
" Never may I commence my song, my due
" To God who best taught song by gift of thee,
" Except with bent head and beseeching hand—
" That still, despite the distance and the dark,
" What was, again my be ; some interchange
" Of grace, some splendor once thy very thought,
" Some benediction anciently thy smile :
"—Never conclude, but raising hand and head
" Thither where eyes, that cannot reach, yet yearn
" For all hope, all sustainment, all reward,
" Their upmost up and on,—so blessing back
" In those thy realms of help, that heaven thy home,

" Some whiteness which, I judge, thy face makes proud,
" Some wanness where, I think, thy foot may fall ! "

Our allegorical friends were united as one man or one woman
in the conviction that " Lyric Love " personfied " Inspiration "
" the Heavenly Muse," etc., and grappled with perfect success
with such expressions as " Boldest of hearts that ever braved.the
" sun," and " human at the red-ripe of the heart," " the summons
" from the darkling earth, " to suffer or to die," " reached thee
amid thy chambers," etc.—while we Realists insisted that it was
an invocation to the spirit of Mrs. Browning in Heaven. The
debate was long and loud, and it was adjourned with divided
honors, as we only possessed the first volume. Before the next
meeting, however, the second had come to hand, and to a crowd-
ed club in breathless silence, I read the concluding words of the
poem:—

" .... Lyric Love,
" Thy rare gold ring of verse (the poet praised)
" Linking our England to this Italy ! "

The uncommon candor of our Allegorical friends was never
more clearly shown than at that moment, when they one and all
gracefully surrendered. When, however, we came to *Childe
Roland to the Dark Tower Came* there was once more a
gathering of the clans, and a beautiful paper was read from
" Unity," which explained in the most complete manner the exact inward significance of the " Cripple," " The old lean horse ;"
the barren land, etc., and reached a magnificent climax in the
undoubted fact, that the " Little bitter brook " meant " Alcohol ! "

The genius of Browning, then, is dramatic. When Pippa
passes, it is just a pure, fresh, loving maiden that passes, and it is
just her sweet young maidenhood that causes her presence and
her voice to charm away the ill demons of lust and hate as she
passes.

And above all, our Pompilia is just God's highest and best
gift to this earth, a pure and noble woman. Our Caponsacchi
is a brave and true man awakening from an ignoble sleep. Our

Pope is a good and grand old man, giving to the world the deep lessons learned in a life spent in doing good.

I cannot even attempt in ten minutes to name those poems of Browning which are dramatic in form. I will simply say a few words about his dramas that are translated from the Greek or are Greek in substance. One conspicuous failure is *Agamemnon*. Two erroneous ideas seem to have been at the bottom of this; one that Æschylus's stately iambics can possibly be represented by the incessant jig of an eleven-syllabled verse, the fact being that our ordinary blank verse is an almost perfect representation of the Greek iambic; the other is the impossible attempt at exact literalness, which, coupled with the use of fantastic words, makes the translation quite as difficult as the original. On the other hand, *Balaustion's Adventure* and *Aristophanes's Apology* must be pronounced a great success.

The second reason for our permanence, which I gave to the younger club, was, that we assigned to each person his work, and that we resolved to pass over no allusion and to leave no difficulty unexplained. In our work on *Aristophanes's Apology* we found that Browning had not only prepared himself for writing by the careful reading of all Aristophanes's plays and all his fragments, but that he had also carefully read the Greek Scholiasts, with their notes on the plays. It was only such thorough work as this, that enabled him to give that astonishing reproduction of Greek life, manners and thought, which renders this part of our poet's work so unique.

S. R. CALTHROP.

SOME OF BROWNING'S BELIEFS.

We meet to-night to commemorate the death of the greatest English writer since Shakspere, the only English writer who can be compared with Shakspere.

> "Shakspere was not our poet, but the world's:
> "Therefore on him no speech ; and brief for thee,
> "Browning. Since Chaucer was alive and hale
> "No man hath walked along our roads with step
> "So active, so inquiring eye, or tongue
> "So varied in discourse."—*Landor.*

"By far the richest nature of our times," says James Russell Lowell.—"It is plain truth to say that no other English poet, "living or dead, Shakspere excepted, has so heaped up human "interest for his readers as has Robert Browning," says the author of " *Obiter Dicta.*" "Mr. Browning exhibits....a "wealth of intellect and a profusion of spiritual insight which we "have been accustomed to find in the pages of Shakspere, and "in those pages only," says Robert Buchanan, in his essays on "Master Spirits."—"We must record at once our conviction "not merely that *The Ring and the Book* is beyond parallel the "supremest poetical achievement of our time," wrote a critic in the *Athenæum,* "but that it is the most precious and profound "spiritual treasure that England has produced since the days of "Shakspere. Its intellectual greatness is as nothing compared "with its transcendent spiritual teaching." Or, as Archdeacon Farrar puts it :

"He has produced not a book but a literature. To have stud-"ied and understood him is a liberal education. With the ex-"ception of Shakspere there is literally no poet, living or dead,

(64)

" in whom we can find so marvellous a portrait-gallery of living
"characters. He has borrowed his jewels from the East and
"from the West; from art, from nature, and from the schools;
"from the classics, the Rabbis, the Renaissance; from Greece,
"Italy, Palestine, France, England, Bagdad, America, Russia;
"from legend and history, from fancy and imagination, from
"kings, paupers, revolutionists, factory-girls, mystic dreamers,
"gay cavaliers, Jews, noble and base, duchesses, musicians,
"poets, painters, dervishes, saints, reformers, heretics; from
"every passion that could ennoble or debase, dilate or contract,
"elevate or ruin the human soul; above all from love; from
"love in every one of its manifestations."

The time has passed for criticisms upon his style, and jokes as
to his intelligibility. "Better say to the first fool who says he
"cannot understand Browning," remarked the Rev. Edward
Everett Hale, "I am sorry for you, but I think I can." Beethoven was in his time called no musician; Chopin said of him
that he had stretched his art to express subjects beyond its range,
till his art ceased to be art. He was told of a certain passage in
one of his works that it was "not allowed." "Then," said he,
"I allow it; let that be its justification." Wagner contended
all his life with such criticism, but who now cares to argue with
those who think the pretty twinklings of Bellini more melodi-
ous? One of Wagner's disciples has drawn a just parallel between his art and Browning's:

"It seems to me that each speaks in a language that he him-
"self has created as a fitting vehicle for the conveyance of his
"thoughts. Each has an individual method of composing and
"working out his theme, and each by his contribution to art has
"substantially widened its sphere and range. * * * One
"more analogy between them is their exaltation, their extasy,
"and the clairvoyance of their unconscious creature instinct that
"was their salient characteristic. They wrote just as this in-
"stinct prompted them; you might disagree with them or agree
"with them, what they sung might be congenial or uncongenial,

" but it must be written or sung.   This is what differentiates
" such men of genius from men of talent.   An idea seizes hold of
" them, and it will not relax its grasp until it is worked out."--
B. L. Mozeley.

Browning himself wrote in 1872 :

" Nor do I apprehend any more charges of being wilfully ob-
" scure, unconscientiously careless, or perversely harsh.   Having
" hitherto done my utmost in the art to which my life is a devo-
" tion, I cannot engage to increase the effort; but I conceive that
" there may be helpful light, as well as re-assuring warmth, in
" the attention and sympathy I gratefully acknowledge."[1]

As has been so often demonstrated, the difficulties in Browning are not in the expression but in the thought.   His are no
poems

> " To turn the page, and let the senses drink
> " A lay that shall not trouble them to think."[2]

" One word on the obscurity of *Sordello*," says Edward Dow-
den.   " It arises not so much from the peculiarities of style. . . .
" as from the unrelaxing demand which is made throughout upon
" the intellectual and imaginative energy and alertness of the
" reader."--Speaking of the *Tomb in St. Praxed's* Ruskin says:
" I know of no other piece of modern English prose or poetry, in
" which there is so much told as in these lines of Renaissance
" spirit.   .   .   .   It is nearly all that I have said of the central
" Renaissance in thirty pages of the ' Stones of Venice.' "[3]--
Swinburne is indignantly emphatic:

. " Now if there is any great quality more perceptible than an-
" other in Mr. Browning's intellect, it is his decisive and incisive
" quality of thought, his sureness and intensity of perception, his
" rapid and trenchant resolution of aim.   To charge him with
" obscurity is about as correct as to call Lynceus purblind, or com-

---

[1] Preface to *Selections.*

[2] Quoted in " *Obiter Dicta.*"

[3] " Modern Painters," IV. 379.

" plain of the slowness of the telegraph wires. He is something
" too much the reverse of obscure ; he is too brilliant and subtle
" for the ready reader of a ready writer to follow with any cer-
" tainty the track of an intelligence which moves with such in-
" cessant rapidity. . . . He never thinks but at full speed ;
" and his rate of thought is to that of another man's as the speed
" of a railway train is to that of a wagon, or the speed of a tele-
" graph to that of a railway."[1]

In considering the form of his poetry we must not forget how
ever-present is his humor, " the last touch and perfection of the
" human faculties," as Carlyle calls it. " The grotesque rhymes
" of Browning," says John Skelton, " like the poetic conceits of
" Shakspere, are merely the holiday frolic of a rich and viva-
" cious imagination." Lowell has said :

" His humor is as genuine as that of Carlyle, and if his mirth
" has not the 'earthquake' character with which Emerson has so
" happily labelled the shaggy merriment of that Jean Paul
" Burns, yet it is always sincere and hearty, and there is a tone
" of meaning in it which always sets us thinking."

So when we miss the point of some apparently uncouth verse,
we may be sure it has for those in closer sympathy with the
poet's thought a special meaning that could not otherwise have
been expressed.

But if he did not write for all, and he did not pretend to or
try to, he gave to those who have found he has something to
say to them a broader, fuller, richer body of verse than is to be
found elsewhere in literature. He was a poet, and among the
half-dozen greatest poets ; but to his disciples he is more than a
poet. A recent Leipzig graduate has published a monograph on
the versification of Pope. He occupies a hundred and forty-
four octavo pages in mathematical calculations of the number of
imperfect rhymes, weak endings, misplaced caesuras to be found
in the writings of this little crooked thing that asked questions.

---

[1] Preface to Works of Marlow.

The work is well done and not without usefulness, but who of us cares to know how often Robert Browning used expressions that would not seem euphonious to Goold Brown?

It is not how he says but what he says that makes Browning's relation to his reader so peculiar. A comparison with the Laureate, so natural in this as in other matters, will illustrate this. Tennyson has reached the heart of all the world. In childhood, in manhood, in age; in self-musing, in love, in bereavement,—even in contemplation of the problems of the day, he has touched almost every chord, and always with a perfection that makes his expression seem the only one adequate. But who of us has learned much from Tennyson? He has given more perfect expression to the thoughts and feelings we have had; he has defined into constellations the nebulae of our consciousness; but have we ever looked upon him as a leader? Take "The Princess," for instance. He treats the question of woman's higher education gracefully, he reaches conclusions that are pedagogically sound, and he has given to many of the arguments a form that can never be surpassed. Yet who quotes Tennyson as an authority on the education of women? Who does not remember less what he said than the perfect way in which he said it?

Now contrast with this the effect of Browning's *Andrea del Sarto*. It is as exquisitely perfect in form, but is that what we remember the poem by? Did it not create for us a personality we can never forget, a criticism that can never be disturbed? Enter any gallery in Europe, and you will find your eye resting on the del Sarto pictures with the peculiar interest that would attach to those painted by a friend. Irresistibly and willingly you find yourself carried back to the studio where the painter,

" often much wearier than you think,"
looked on

" My face, my moon, my everybody's moon,
" Which everybody looks on and calls his,
" And, I suppose, is looked on by in turn,
" While she looks—no one's: very dear, no less!"

Not all the critics that have ever written can affect the view of the painter and his works that Browning has fixed within you.

Where else out of Shakspere are there men and women so real as those of Browning?   Go to Rome, and where Cæsar and Augustus and Nero are names to you, Pompilia is a person. You look in your guide-book for the historical associations that linger about the great monuments of the world's history, and feel that you are conscientiously supplementing your study of the past.   But when you pass down Via Vittoria, the " aspectable street" where Pompilia lived, it needs no effort to look for

> " the poor Virgin that I used to know
> " At our street corner in a lonely niche,—
> " The babe that sat upon her knees, broke off,—
> " Thin white glazed clay, you pitied her the more :
> "She, not the gay ones, always got my rose." [1]

Among all the memories of the square near by you do not forget the

> " foreigner had trained a goat,
> " A shuddering white woman of a beast,
> " To climb up, stand straight on a pile of sticks
> " Put close, which gave the creature room enough :
> " When she was settled there he, one by one,
> " Took away all the sticks, left just the four
> " Whereon the little hoofs did really rest ;
> " There she kept firm, all underneath was air." [1]

And when you come to San Lorenzo in Lucina, you recollect it not as containing the tomb of Nicholas Poussin, but as Pompilia's

> "own particular place."

You stand by the altar rail and give the sexton his lira to uncurtain Guido's Crucifixion, but what you fix in mind is that this was the scene of that unhappy marriage.

> " However I was hurried through the storm,
> " Next dark eve of December's deadest day—

---

[1] *Ring and the Book.*

" How it rained !—through our street and the Lion's mouth,
" And the bit of Corso,—cloaked round, covered close,
" I was like something strange or contraband,—
" Into blank San Lorenzo, up the aisle,
" My mother keeping hold of me so tight,
" I fancied we were come to see a corpse
" Before the altar which she pulled me toward.
" There were found waiting an unpleasant priest
" Who proved to be the brother, not our parish friend,
" But one with mischief-making mouth and eye,
" Paul, whom I know since to my cost.   And then
" I heard the heavy church-door lock out help
" Behind us : for the customary warmth
" Two tapers shivered on the altar. 'Quick—
"'Lose no time!' cried the priest.   And straightway down
" From .. what's behind the altar where he hid—
" Hawk-nose and yellowish and bush and all,
" Stepped Guido, caught my hand, and there was I
" O' the chancel and the priest had opened book,
" Read here and there, made me say that and this,
" And after, told me I was now a Wife." [1]

Browning has done more than merely to show us these men and women. He has shown them to us in the crises of their histories. "My stress lay on the incidents in the development "of a soul : little else is worth study," he says in his preface to *Sordello*.

> " The soul itself,
> " Its shifting fancies and celestial lights,
> " With all its grand orchestral silences
> " To keep the pauses of the rhythmic sounds." [2]

He deals with real things, never with the vague and incoherent images that some call fancy. Whatever he writes

> " if cut down the middle

---

[1] *Ring and the Book.*

[2] Mrs. Browning's " Aurora Leigh."

"Shows a heart within blood-tinctured, of a veined
"humanity." [1]

He realizes the saying of Goethe, "The poet should seize
" the particular, and he should if there be anything sound thus
"represent the universal." ; and that of Matthew Arnold :

" More and more mankind will discover that we have to turn
" to poetry to interpret life for us, to console and sustain us.
" Science will appear incomplete without it, for well does Words-
" worth call poetry the impassioned expression which is in the
" countenance of all science, the breath and finer spirit of knowl-
" edge."

What of the universal has he especially represented to us ? In
other words, what are the beliefs that we may especially charac-
terize as Browning's?

I. In the first place *he believes in Life*—life in this world, in
our day and generation. You never think of him as
        "sicklied o'er with the pale cast of thought."

"He is so unmistakably and deliciously alive," says the author
of *Obiter Dicta*, and Arthur Symons expands the thought :

" Of all poets Mr. Browning is the healthiest and manliest ; he
" is one of the 'substantial men' of whom Landor speaks. His
" genius is robust with vigorous blood, and his tone has the cheeri-
" ness of intellectual health. The most subtle of minds, his is
" the least sickly. The wind that blows on his pages is no hot
" and languorous breeze, laden with scents and sweets, but a
" fresh salt wind blowing in from the sea. His poetry is a tonic,
" it braces and invigorates. '*Il fait vivre ses phrases*,' his verses
" live and throb with life. He is incomparably plentiful of vital
" heat, so thoroughly and delightfully alive." [2]

Browning says in *Saul* :

" How good is man's life, the mere living ! how fit to employ,
" All the heart and the soul and the senses forever in joy."

---

[1] Mrs. Browning's "Lady Geraldine's Courtship."

[2] "Introduction to the Study of Browning," 1886.

And in *At the Mermaid :*

> " Have you found your life distasteful ?
> " My life did and does smack sweet.
> " Was your youth of pleasure wasteful ?
> " Mine I saved, and hold complete.
> " Do your joys with age diminish ?
> " When mine fail me, I'll complain.
> " Must in death your daylight finish ?
> " My sun sets to rise again."

" To blend a profound knowledge of human nature, a keen
" perception of the awful problem of human destiny, with the
" conservation of a joyous human spirit, to know and not despair
" of them, to battle with one's spiritual foes and not be burdened
" by them, is given only to the very strong.   This is to be a val-
" iant and unvanquished soldier of humanity."[1]

II. In the second place, *he is the poet of the Positive Virtues.*
His St. Peter would ask of men not whether they had smoked
cigarettes, but whether they had accomplished anything in life.
" Do something, produce something. . . in God's name," cried
Carlyle.   Mrs. Oliphant chose a happy title for her " *Makers* of
" Florence."   Browning puts the emphasis on accomplishment.

> " Do thy day's work, dare
> " Refuse no help thereto, since help refused
> " Is hindrance sought and found.   Win but the race
> " Who shall object, ' He tossed there wine cups off,
> " ' And, just at starting, Lilith kissed his lips.' "

His favorite among the gods is Hercules.   What if he reason :

> " Count the day-by-day
> " Existence thine, and all the other chance !
> " Ay, and pay homage also to, by far
> " The sweetest of divinities for man,
> " Kupris ! Benignant goddess will she prove !
> " But as for all else, leave and let things be ! "

---

[1] " Edinburgh Review," July, 1869.

This Browning can forgive, for Hercules had
   " the authentic sign and seal
" Of Godship, that it ever waxes glad
" And more glad, until gladness blossoms, bursts
" Into a rage to suffer for mankind. " [1]

    " God
" Ne'er dooms to waste the strength he deigns impart." [2]

" 'Tis work for work's sake that man's needing." [3]

" All service ranks the same with God." [4]

   " Then welcome each rebuff
   " That turns earth's smoothness rough,
" Each sting that bids, nor sit nor stand, but go !
   " Be our joys three parts pain !
   " Strive and hold cheap the strain !
" Learn, nor account the pang !   Dare, never grudge
   the throe ! " [5]

   " I count life just a stuff
" To try the soul's strength on." [6]

   " When the fight begins with himself
" A man's worth something." [7]

" How carve way in the life that lies before
" If bent on groaning ever for the past ? " [1]

Even if the end be base, better vigorously strive for it than
weakly and aimlessly long for it.
  " I hear your reproach—' But delay was best,
  " ' For their end was a crime ! '—Oh, a crime will do
  " As well, I reply, to serve for a test,
  " As a virtue golden through and through.
  " Let a man contend to the uttermost
  " For his life's set prize, be it what it may !

---

[1] *Balaustion's Adventure.*   [2] *Paracelsus.*   [3] *Pacchiarotto.*
[4] *Pippa Passes.*   [5] *Rabbi Ben Ezra.* [6] *In a Balcony.* [7] *Bishop
Blougram's Apology.*

" And the sin I impute to each frustrate ghost,
" Was the unlit lamp and the ungirt loin,
" Though the end in sight was a crime I say." [1]

Here it is not as Stedman supposes [2] —Stedman, who thinks *The Ring and the Book* began to show the decadence of Browning's powers!—that Browning means to justify adultery, but that for this couple an earnest effort of any kind would have been a step upward.

III. In the third place, *he judges men by their Effort, not by their Accomplishment.*

" 'Tis not what man Does that exalts him, but what man
    Would do." [3]

" What I aspired to be
" And was not, comforts me." [4]

Who shall say what insurmountable obstacles prevented attainment here?

" A tree born to erectness of bole,
" Palm, or plane or pine, we laud if lofty, columnar—
" Little if athwart, askew,—leave to the axe and the flame!
" Where is the vision may penetrate earth and beholding acknowledge
" Just one pebble at root ruined the straightness of stem ?
" Whose fine vigilance follows the sapling, accounts for the failure,
" Here blew wind, so it bent; there the sun lodged, so it broke." [5]

No other writer that I know carries this thought so far.

" Ever judge of men by their professions! For tho'
" bright moment of promising is but a moment and cannot be
" prolonged, yet, if sincere in its moment's extravagant goodness,
" why, trust it, and know the man by it, I say—not by his per-

---

[1] *The Statue and the Bust.*   [2] " Victorian Poets."   [3] *Saul.*
[4] *Rabbi Ben Ezra.*   [5] *Ixion.*

" formance—which is half the world's work, interfere, as the
" world needs must with its accidents and circumstances,—the
" profession was purely the man's own!   I judge people by what
" they might be,—not are nor will be." [1]

" There grows in each heart as in a shrine,
" The giant image of Perfection." [2]

" If ye demur, this judgment on your head,
" Never to reach the ultimate, angel's law,
" Indulging every instinct of the soul,
" There where law, life, joy, impulse are one thing!" [3]

IV. Nay, *it is Man's distinctive blessing that he cannot reach
Perfection here.* Goodness is not position, but direction of
motion.

" Finds progress, man's distinctive mark alone,
" Not God's and not the beasts': God is, they are,
" Man partly is, and wholly hopes to be." [3]

" They are perfect,—how else? they shall never change,
" We are faulty—why not? we have time in store." [4]

" Imperfection means perfection hid,
" Reserved in part, to grace the after time." [5]

" A man's reach should exceed his grasp,
" Or what's a heaven for?" [6]

" But what's whole, can increase no more,
" Is dwarfed and dies, since here's its sphere." [7]

" Better have failed in the high aim, as I,
" Than vulgarly in the low aim succeed,
" As, God be thanked, I do not!" [8]

" That low man seeks a little thing to do,
" Sees it and does it;
" This high man with a great thing to pursue,
" Does ere he knows it.

---

[1] *A Soul's Tragedy.*   [2] *Paracelsus.*   [3] *A Death in the Desert.*
[4] *Old Pictures in Florence.*   [5] *Cleon.*   [6] *Andrea del Sarto.*
[7] *Dis Aliter Visum.*   [8] *Inn Album.*

" That low man goes on adding one to one,
  " His hundred's soon hit:
" This high man, aiming at a million,
  " Misses an unit:
" That, has the world here—should he need the next,
  " Let the world mind him !
" This, turns himself on God, and unperplexed,
  " Seeking, shall find Him."[1]

" St. John's discourse concludes with words which are an
" epitome of Mr. Browning's religious faith as we recognize it in
" many of his other writings. Man's life consists in never-ceas-
" ing progress. The god-like power is imparted to him gradu-
" ally, and step by step he approaches nearer to absolute truth
"—to divine perfection. But in this mortal life the goal can
" never be attained : the ideal which he strives to realize here
" exists only in heaven, and awaits him as a reward of all his
" faithful efforts."[2]

V. Hence, *Browning is a firm believer in Immortality.* Tennyson says in " In Memoriam."

  " Oh yet we trust that *somehow* good
    " Will be the final goal of ill,
    " To pangs of nature, sins of will,
  " Defects of doubt, and taints of blood.
  " That nothing walks with aimless feet:
    " That not one life shall be destroyed,
    " Or cast as rubbish to the void
  " When God hath made the pile complete."

Contrast this with the steadfast faith of *Abt Vogler :*

  " There shall never be one lost good ! What was shall
    live as before,
  " The evil is null, is naught, is silence implying sound ;
  " What was good shall be good, with, for evil, so much
    good more ;

---

[1] *A Grammarian's Funeral.*
[2] Mrs. M. G. Glazebrook.

" On the earth the broken arcs; in the heaven a per-
    fect round."

" The In Memoriam utterances sound like the voice of Mr.
" Little Faith, after listening to Mr. Greatheart in such a defiance
" of evil as this,"—says Edward Berdoe.   Browning " is the poet
" of the Gothic—agony and harmony in unity, agony working
" itself at last to a place in the great harmony of the whole,"
says E. Paxton Hood.

    " Why rushed the discords in, but that harmony should
        " be prized?"[1]

Love is beneath all,
        "as some implied chord subsists,
    " Steadily underlies the accidental mists
    " Of music springing thence, that run their mazy race
        around." [2]

            "I have faith such end shall be;
                " From the first, Power was—I knew.
            " Life has made clear to me
                " That, strive but for closer view,
            " Love were as plain to see."
                    " This world's no blot for us,
            "Nor blank : it means intensely, and means good.
            " To find its meaning is my meat and drink." [3]

    " Earth changes, but thy soul and God stand sure." [4]

In this age of doubt, when men are so proud of their uncer-
tainty that they give a name to it and call themselves Agnostics,
what a blessing there is in these utterances of a mind so gifted ;
of whom that other great mind of this generation, George
Eliot, said:

---

[1] *Abt Vogler.*
[2] *Fifine at the Fair.*
[3] *Fra Lippo Lippi.*
[4] *Rabbi Ben Ezra.*

" To be a poet is to have a soul so quick to discern that no
" shade of quality escapes it, and so quick to feel that discern-
" ment is but a hand playing with finely ordered variety on the
" chord of emotion ; a soul in which knowledge passes instantly
" into feeling, and feeling flashes back as a new organ of
"knowledge."

C. W. BARDEEN.

REMARKS BY REV. C. DeB. MILLS.

Mr. C. DeB. Mills, though not on the programme, was called upon by the Chairman, and spoke substantially as follows :

We have been hearing, here to-night, Mr. Chairman, the testimony drawn in careful statement of students, critics, in their several lines of research, of this poet and philosopher. These have all spent years in the reading and study of the various and many things he has given to the public. They have furnished us their thoughtful, deliberate estimate, and pointed out to us so clearly, so instructively the grounds they base it on. We have been enriched, enlarged, and quickened exceedingly.

What can *I* say now? What have I any right to attempt to say? I am not, have never been a student of this poet, as I am sorry to own. My acquaintance with his writings is very superficial. I can give you at best but my rough impression, a judgment crude, partial doubtless, certainly far inadequate, of this venerated and now sainted name.

I readily believe that Browning was a great lyric and dramatic poet. The strong statements of his cotemporaries, men themselves of great eminence in their respective fields of letters, some of which were kindred with his,—such men as Carlyle, Landor, Ruskin, Dickens, Lowell, etc., suffice for testimony that should be conclusive to us, that there was eminent merit in this man. It is related of Carlyle by his most recent biographer, Dr. Garnett, that sincerely wishing to compliment Browning on his signal performance in writing *The Ring and the Book*, he said to him :

"It is a wonderful book, one of the most wonderful poems "ever written. I re-read it all through—all made out of an Old

(79)

" Bailey story that might have been told in ten lines, and only
" wants forgetting."

This was the highest tribute the brusque Scotsman knew to
pay his honored friend, however equivocal the quality of a portion of it may seem to us. Landor spoke of him as "a great
poet, a very great poet indeed, as the world will "have to agree
" with us in thinking."

A rare fortune has befallen this man, without precedent in
modern times,—and these are the only times in which there
could have been a precedent,— in that during his own life time,
numerous Societies have been formed, devoted supreme and sole
to the study of this writer, the attempt to penetrate, to interpret,
to apprehend his often difficult, sometimes enigmatic poems.
Wherever the English-speaking peoples are, there are the Browning Societies, composed of the brightest, most intelligent and
thoughtful in their several communities, religiously dedicated to
these studies, and feeling themselves, I doubt not, well rewarded
for all the labor they bestow. Never, so far as I know, has
such fortune come to any author before. It shows that Browning has already spoken to his own time and age, has delivered a
message that a multitude are eager to hear.

I have frankly to own that some things I have found in the
reading of this poet, have not met my own thought, and have
had the effect to reduce rather than heighten the attraction I have
felt to him. He seems to rest in an optimism, which to some of
us would seem disproportionate, excessive, verging towards if
not touching indifferentism, and which would bear to a tame
sleepy acquiescence in all things about us as they are, irrespec-
tive of the agency of man to amend and to save. He appears
at times to break down, to obliterate all distinction of character,
and essentially to say to us that the broad way and the narrow
both bring up at the same goal. I suppose it is what we have in
Emerson, as he expresses himself sometimes in very bold statement, "Man though in brothels, or jails, or on gibbets, is on his
" way to all that is good and true." If I understand Browning
in some of his utterances, he seems to carry as far.

I am well aware that there is a side of truth in all this decla-
ration of an exceeding optimism. "God," says Plutarch,
"is the brave man's hope, and not the coward's excuse." There
are hours when we must rest sole, final, in the absolute assurance
that there is a Rule supreme, far higher, wholly beyond all we
can see, which is doing all things to infinite ends of excellence,
bringing accord out of discord, order out of chaos, good out of
evil, drawing nourishment from very poison, making all the sin,
wickedness we see, subserve finally the highest and best. I know
of no act of worship more genuine, more pure, than is done when
the soul in midst of its severe stress and trial, sorrow, suffering,
breavement, darkness of solitude that knows no ray of light, dis-
cerns no solace, no providence, or good or justice at all, lays
itself naked on the bosom of the infinite Truth and Love, and
feels, ejaculates from deepest depths within, "All things are well,
"and *shall* be well."

But that lazy optimism, and sleepy indifferentism, which con-
founds all moral distinction, abolishes the ideal, which makes
Jesus and Judas essentially one, which sees all conduct the same,
all types of character identical in their quality, all men alike hasten-
ing forward with best endeavor to the goal of their being, nothing left for human effort to do to mend, correct, meliorate,—is
pusillanimous, treasonable, false to nature and to man. It makes
God the coward's excuse, is relaxing to tone, and demoralizing to
the energies of the being within. I have been in communities
where such optimists and dreamers dwell, and have heard them
described as among the most characterless, invincibly renunciant,
inert, and worthless of mortals. So far as any endeavor in slight-
est degree for improvement of their neighborhood, or of society,
was concerned in any respect whatever, they might have been
just as well in Dahomey, or on another planet. They have
drunken deep of that cup which Browning sometimes pours.
"A too rapid unification, and an excessive appliance to parts and
"particulars," says Emerson, "are the twin dangers of specula-
"tion." A too rapid unification it is in sphere of the practical,

which ignores the fact of conflict in this world of Time, and
deadens, stifles in the mind, the mandate of moral appeal.
Sooner, infinitely sooner than that torpor and renunciation of
duty, I would hear with stunning emphasis the iteration perpetual
of Kant's 'Categorical Imperative,' would have for us all, the
Sinai thunders and terrific lightning flashes of Carlyle's denun-
ciation and drastic summons to gird up and do, to fight a man's
battle for God, for the claim of high Heaven and the Supreme
Justice in this false and maddened world. This is stimulating,
medicinal, wakes and rouses the torpid, slumbering energies;
bidding the man out to conflict, to the exposures and the perils of
the fight; that is soporific, relaxing, lulls to death. Ariston,
Plutarch tells us, was wont to say that "neither a bath nor a lec-
"ture served any purpose unless it were purgative."

Browning was not such a renunciant; he was no deserter or
coward. He incites to the following of the high behests; summons each to be up and do. The one sin he finds that stains
and stings with mortal taint the individual, is permitting to himself to live and end the life with the " unlit lamp and the ungirt
"loin." A man cannot do this, inciting every one to reach his
utmost best, holding up the immense sanctions that overarch
human conduct, without affirming in implication that there is a
difference pronounced, vital, between the worthy and unworthy,
true and false, good and bad. That he seems at times to blend
all, carrying his optimism to such point as apparently to imply
the indifference, the substantial identity of all conduct, all character, is to my view a limitation, a fault in Browning. It abates
from the virile quality of the man. Emerson speaking of the
writings of Plato, remarks that he is always literary, never otherwise. There is " regnancy of intellect," so absolute as to be vir-
tually sole in his work, and hence " his writings have not the
" vital authority which the screams of prophets and the sermons
" of unlettered Arabs and Jews possess." There is no power that
takes and holds, commands the person, be he who he may, as
does the moral appeal, presenting, pressing the ideal claim of

sovereign law. I think I have read writers, who in their inspiring to lofty character, in rousing, impelling, setting on fire for the attainment of highest, best, in royal endeavor, and sublime self-sacrifice, were superior to Browning, though in genius much inferior to him.

But I remember that our brilliant historian and philosopher, not long since passed away, unequalled in his delineations of character, and unexcelled in his affirmation of the moral, at the close of his masterly essay upon Mirabeau, calls our attention to three moral reflections that he draws from his subject:—" Moral " reflection *third* and last,—that neither thou nor we, good reader, " had any hand in the making of this Mirabeau ;—else who knows "but we had objected, in *our* wisdom ? But it was the Upper " Powers that made him, without once consulting us ; they and "not we, so and not otherwise." Browning is what he is, by temperament and constitution ; his endowment is so and not otherwise. We must take him as he is, and see what he has of value for *us*.

I believe the reader must see that for one thing he has a singular, an exceptional appreciation of *the divineness of womanhood*. This seems to mark him as almost *sui generis*, and sole among all the writers of our age that I know ; it puts him on elevated plane when measured beside any of the great writers of history. He has penetrated these depths, he knows woman's soul, he reads her tender, sensitive, sweet nature, her possibilities with all this of brave heroic character. In *The Ring and the Book* he has given a lofty and most touching ideal :—this girl, this child, of parentage unknown but guilty, drawn originally as would appear from one of the slums of Rome, bound over, sold, while yet but a child, in pretended marriage to a brute, so sheer, so unqualified, that there is scarcely in the whole man one relieving feature,—a character of " pure cussedness," as is sometimes said among us,— enslaved in a relation to which she was no party, and wherein there was nothing not revolting to nature, subjected there to unnamed wrong and outrage, in the end murdered at Guido's hand,

and passing out of life with a testimony on her lips of highest nobleness, supreme generosity of soul, a sweetness of affection and compassion for her enemies and murderers like that of the dying Jesus for his foes.

"To keep tenderness," says an ancient Chinese Sage, "I pro- "nounce strength." "The weakest thing," he declares, "Shall "gallop over the strongest." "And I, if I be lifted up," says Jesus, "will draw all men to me." This character of such divine celestial qualities as Browning gives Pompilia, union and blending of both tenderness and strength, he must have realized to portray, must have acquired to be able to describe. He had been that, had become in thought, in soul experience, that woman. "The soul," says Prof. Newman, "must become a woman." It was because he had percurred this experience in his own life and being, that he could afford us this lofty ideal in the Pompilia he presents, certainly one of the most touching, most inspiring, ex- alted characters that have ever been depicted by bard and poet in any age of history.

He acquired this fine delicate appreciation, reading of the noblest rich qualities of the soul, and appropriation of them in his own being, through his acquaintance with one woman. No one can doubt that his meeting with Elizabeth Barrett marked an epoch in the life for him. From this he could date, it opened an era new and memorable evermore. Her presence and spirit unsealed all the deep fountains of his being, waked the silent flame into song, revealed the divineness of womanhood, and made him henceforth in this appreciation a full man. "That "male and female should dwell together," says Mencius, "is the "greatest of human relations." This woman was Mentor, lode star, Madonna to Browning; he received new birth through her. Read the invocations to her his "Lyric Love," in *The Ring and the Book*, as he offers his tribute :—

—"My due
"To God who best taught song by gift of thee,"—
and in other of his writings, and you shall see what this pure

exalted soul, this royal type of womanhood was and ever remained to him. Through her he could see, by her inspiration and steady uplift he was gifted with the power to depict and bring alive before us, so that we too saw and felt the divine qualities of character he shows incarnate in his Pompilia.

"In thy face," said the dying Bunsen, looking up into the countenance of his wife,—"in thy face have I beheld the "Eternal." Through her, the maiden. the wife, the mother, Browning saw; he read the symbolism, all the world was laid open to him, he apprehended, appreciated women, men, children, all mankind, and great Nature besides. "He that having the "masculine nature," says Lao Tsze, "knows at same time to "keep the feminine nature, shall be the whole world's channel."

We must say he was *learned in the lore of love.* He had read deep, had had an inmost experience, and it finds utterance in all that he speaks and does. He had had an experience, and that experience wrote on all his nature, transformed, quickened, and new made all his being. He became the sweet singer of this sentiment, not on earthly plane simply, but on the spiritual, the eternal. Love is the one theme to which the mind never grows old, we never weary hearing its story; when it carries to the heights of pure, spiritual devotion of one to another, of man to woman, woman to man, it is forever supremely engaging and inspiring. Read *By the Fireside*, and there see what sweet, tender, exalted affection his was, so reverent, unselfish to point of self-abnegating, as he describes in reminiscence the lone walk of the two together in the solitary gorge as the night shadows were falling, the presence of the still, unused, dilapidated temple, the looking down of the mute trees upon them, and the silent speech audible to the inner ear, the mingling together of the two souls in this communion, and the coming of the moment, the fleeting fugitive instant, that was the critical, the eventful one for him, that had in its keeping his fortune, his fate, for life, and the manner and way in which he fronted and met it. Nothing should take from him the reverence due to personality, nothing tempt him to swerve from that sentiment of perfect respect and religious deference to the judgment, the will of that other, which must be left unapproached by so much as a breath that might influence or sway the scale in decision to the result he desires.   The soul palpitates with anxious hope, with eager tense solicitude, but it must not suffer its least wish to invade, to touch the precincts of the sacred autonomy of that true, that upright and lofty heart.   It is beautiful, exalted above the plane of all our common, I might say our uncommon, our exceptionally good and superior life, in society.   Who of us has recognized and honored such an ideal in his moments of passionate devotion, in his addresses and wooing, and putting the question to the maiden of his love?   As Confucius is reported to have said to one of his disciples in regard to the great Law of Reciprocity in conduct, or as we term it the Golden Rule, "Tsze, "you have not attained to that"; so may Browning say certainly to most of us, in reference to this norm for man.

An ideal union it was, the celestial marriage on earth.   The two persons, each distinct, autonomic, itself to the end, yet melted and blended gloriously into one.   Sir Joshua Reynolds said, "I feel a self-congratulation in knowing myself capable of "such sensations as he (Angelo) intended to excite."   We may feel self-congratulation if we may find ourselves capable of the sentiments, the stir of quickening and the aspiration Browning intended to excite in the pictures, as he draws them for us in lineaments of beauty all his own, of the true love.

I have sometimes thought of him in regard to this matter of the sentiment in comparison with Goethe, whom we all know to have been one of the transcendent geniuses and great poets of the world.   Professor Harris has characterized his works as suggestive beyond the works of all other writers.   Mrs. Shorey, in an excellent article she has written of him,[1] describes Goethe

---

[1] On the "Elective Affinities," a paper read before the Milwaukee Literary School in August, 1886.   Published in the "Poetry and Philosophy of Goethe," Chicago, 1887.

as "very specially the poet of women." "No other poet has "given us so many types of womanly perfection and graces." On the side of the tender sentiment, Goethe was very richly endowed. "Of a poetic, feeling-full nature," says Calvert of him. But that sentiment went out exuberantly, it became wild, unregulated, especially in the earlier years, the morning manhood of the poet, and he fell deeply, passionately in love many and many a time. The affection he indulged was allowed to be illicit, and brought him seeds and fruitage of bitter sorrow. His weakness, we may almost say, came of his greatness, in that he was so exceptionally dowered on the side of the affectional; his greatness fell short of the true and highest conquest, and thus descended, lapsed to weakness, hard for us to condone in such a man. If, as Carlyle says, he "climbed the craggy "heights,"—and I think we must believe that,—it was through pain, manifold suffering, sorrow, remorse.

We find Browning not like our poet in regard to this early experience of infirmity and sin. His nature, too, had the passional, he was a lover, warm, ardent, o'erflowing, but it was a regulated affection, a loyal, lofty passion. It had in it self-abnegation, willingness to make the high surrender, a supreme reverence for personality, and devotion chivalric to the end, of his soul to one. Warm as was his love, it was noble and pure, ardent as the affection, it was always superior, of celestial type and quality. Goethe must take his place below, he stands not his equal here.

I have sometimes thought of him beside Emerson, our great American sage, philosopher, poet, too. Emerson had loves, but they seem to have been largely impersonal, if I may so say. In respect to persons, in respect to women, his nature appears not to have been full-dowered as was that of either of the names just referred to. The affections, it has been said, were imprisoned in the intellect. All emotion was saturated and in a degree dissolved in pure thought. He was in temperament calm, poised, self-centred. To great extent he was always self-fed. The man who could write, "I love man but not men;" who could say,

"The soul knows no persons," you would not expect to be deeply, certainly not overpoweringly drawn in his relations to any.
He communed with ideas, walked in companionship with inner
and invisible. I opine that his soul in the deeper depths was a
casket that no man, no woman ever opened, a shrine that no eye
ever beheld save his own. The seen was everywhere transpar-
ent to him. He views others as hints of a possibility not yet
realized. In any bereavement he cannot be vitally bereft; his
eye looks ever upward and beyond. He sees always the silver
lining in the cloud, and reads the compensations, the great medi-
ations in nature, the supreme beneficence that presides over all.
His heart is staid, restful, at repose everywhere.

There was an element of the incommunicable in his nature; he
could not impart himself as he fain would with fullness, with
freedom to others,—no, not even his intimates. In the confi-
dences with himself which he commits to his journal he says,—
"Strange it is that I can go back to no part of youth, no past
"relation without shrinking and shrinking. Not Ellen, not Ed-
"ward, not Charles. Infinite compunctions embitter each of
"these dear names, and all who surrounded them." He mourns
that he was not made, like these beatified mates of his, super-
ficially generous and noble as well as internally so. Dr. Holmes
says of him, "Emerson is a citizen of the universe who has taken
"up his residence for a few days and nights in this travelling
"caravansery between the two inns that hang out the signs of
"Venus and Mars. This little planet could not provincialize
"such a man."

Serene, spotless sage he, opulent and generous, enriching with
his solid sparkling wisdom,—ingots unnumbered of pure imperish-
able gold,—the present and the coming ages, perhaps beyond any
other man of the century. He abode for a time on earth, but
was primarily not of earth, so exalted in his thought, so pronounced and fixed in his idealism, dwelling in the transcendent,
his devotion sole upon that "high divine beauty that can be loved
"without effeminacy." He seems here not to belong to the world

of Time, not to be one like ourselves, with the affections, sentiment, passions of mortal men.

Emerson was ethereal, Browning mundane, while also elevated
and ideal. Emerson lived mainly in the intellectual, Browning
with intellect large, exceptionally generous and great in endowment, had united sentiment, warmth, ardor, flowing out lyrically
in expression of a most vital and intense love. Emerson, so raised
his eye, so empyrean his vision, looked beyond the personal,
knew not persons ; Browning, denizen of earth, to which he
grappled as one belonging there, looked around as eager to know,
to appropriate all, fastened to person, by whose presence he was
inspired and lifted to his loftiest, sweetest utterances in verse.
Browning had no impediment that withheld him from the free
fitting expression of his inner, glowing self. Browning on the
side of the affectional, comes nearer, stands closer, is more helpful than Emerson. He in this regard occupied higher vantage, is
more inspiring and uplifting to us than Goethe.

Shall we not hope, shall we not believe, that the two souls
that were so near and so much to each other, were life, quickening, and fresh accession of power each to each, disparted by the
too early death of the cherished mate, have now again in the
eternities and immensities of God, become united and one,
never to be separated more? Shall we not believe that he, sore
bereft, left lone, to whom the earth wherever visited, and how
bright soever with its companionships and affections, was still
one great solitude, who,—like the forlorn necessitous prince in
Goethe's *Tale of Tales*, deprived of half his nature, shorn of
the best of himself, wandering wide and far searching through
all lands for the Fair Lily that should restore and make him
whole,—was himself also a mourner and a seeker, has now gained
his "Lyric Love, soul half-angel and half-bird," and henceforth
in the embrace and companionship of her sweet being, is to reach
ever up with her to new heights of wisdom, possession, power,
reading through the symbol to the substance, through personal
to reality transcendent of person, beyond and above any and all

we know; through the qualities we see, to that, the One we do
not see, approximating forever through this staircase of symbol
to the illimitable, the infinite Truth and Beauty and Love?

> "Think, when our one soul understands
>   "The great Word which makes all things new—
> "When earth breaks up and Heaven expands—
>   "How will the change strike me and you
> "In the House not made with hands?"
> "Oh, I must feel your brain prompt mine,
>   "Your heart anticipate my heart,
> "You must be just before, in fine,
>   "See and make me see, for your part,
> "New depths of the Divine!"

NOTES OF A CALL ON MR. BROWNING.

In January, 1884, I happened to be in London at the time when Mr. Browning, having recently finished *Ferishta's Fancies*, had visited his son in Paris, and come on to Warwick Crescent for a time. I wrote to him, asking if as a representative of the Syracuse Browning Club I might be permitted to call upon him, and received the reply of which a photographed facsimile is printed facing the title-page of this volume, the only change being that in his note the crest was upon the flap of the envelope.

Warwick Crescent was off the Edgeware Road, near Paddington, in a locality not particularly pleasant: a four-story house at the end of a long brick block. Without taking up my card a maid ushered me at once up two pairs of stairs to the famous drawing-room that so many Browningites remember fondly. This extended the length of the house, and was filled with furniture so various that one readily surmised most of the articles must have individual histories. Some tapestry hung from the wall, a grand piano occupied much of the front room, and Mr. Browning, who greeted me cordially, drew up two comfortable green chairs before the grate.

He began the conversation, like the rest of the world, by complaining of the weather, saying it seemed different enough to come to London, where he was told the sun had not been seen in fourteen days, from Venice, where for weeks the sky had been unclouded, and the nightingales were singing. He asked if we had the nightingale in America, said there was an American artist in Venice who painted his robins as big as young pigeons, and wondered if robins were really as large as that with us. He spoke of the American lady whose guest he had been in Venice, saying that he had known duchesses and princesses, but never hostess more royal in her hospitality. To my surprise, he told me he received no royalty upon the edition of his works published in Boston, and had never even seen it. They had paid him something upon the first volumes issued, but owing to some disagreement with the London publishers had not continued it.

I asked him about the new cheap edition of his works that had been announced, and he said he was afraid Mr. Furnivall had interrupted that project by excessive zeal, putting a note into the " Academy " about a shilling edition we ought to have.

" And you know," he went on to say, " a shilling edition of " *my* works would never pay. It is different with Tennyson. " He began a little before I did, but his poems took the public by " storm. They appeal to everybody at the first glance, while " mine have to be studied into."

I said it was perhaps partly because we had to study into them that those of us who took that pains felt such peculiar interest in them ; and that if one could judge from the Browning societies springing up everywhere the number who felt they must have the help he gave was increasing rapidly.

Looking musingly into the fire, his legs stretched out, and his hands in his trowsers pockets, he replied at some length :

" Whatever popularity my books have," he said, " if that term " can yet be applied to them at all, has grown up within a very few " years. I have waited long enough for it. I have always felt "there was something in them, and I have had a small but "constant and eminent band of adherents. Why, years and " years ago, a man who stands very high—well as high as any " critic—wrote to me : 'Now, my dear Browning, I tell you *in* "' *strict confidence* that'—never mind what, but he expressed a "judgment so gratifying that if he had but said a quarter of it "aloud it would have done me a world of good with the public. " But I have had to wait for that."

I remarked that with us at home it was not merely as a literary luxury, but as a practical help in the difficult problems of life that we had seized upon his books with such eagerness. We felt personally grateful to him quite as much as a philosopher as a poet. He seemed interested in what I told him of our club, particularly of the effect it had had in bringing into religious and moral sympathy those whose creeds had been named so differently that they had supposed themselves chasms apart. He even encouraged me to describe at some length a meeting held the winter before at Bishop Huntington's, where Methodist and Unitarian, Presbyterian and Catholic, Episcopal and Agnostic vied in seeking for points of agreement instead of points of dissension.

But when I asked him as to an interpretation, I found him singularly forgetful of his own best work. We had battled together over the line,

"Sirs, I obeyed,"

in Caponsacchi's tale of his conversion. At first most of us had thought it was Pompilia he obeyed, and had been quite impatient when Mr. Mundy had insisted that it was not Pompilia but the Church. One by one, however, we had most of us come around to Mr. Mundy's way of thinking, and now we should be glad to be assured by the poet himself that we were right.

He listened indulgently, but replied that the fact was he had not read *The Ring and the Book* since he wrote it, and he did not remember that particular passage; but *from my statement of the context* (!) he should think it must be the Church Caponsacchi obeyed: in fact he was certain of it; it couldn't have been Pompilia. But it was long since he had seen the book. The Browning Society [1] had given him a set of all his works,

---

[1] Browning kept clear of our society, and we kept clear of him. But when we couldn't understand a passage or a poem, I either walkt or wrote to him, and got his explanation of it. At first I didn't take the volume with me, and he amused me very much by saying, "'Pon my word I don't know what I *did* mean by "the poem. I gave away my last copy six years ago, and I "haven't seen a line of it since. But I'll borrow a copy to-mor-

but so elegantly bound that he had not wanted to have them about till he changed his residence, and in fact he had never opened them to the light. He was soon to sell this house to a railway-company that wanted to erect a station here; and when he moved into a larger one, these books should have a prominent place. In fact, he would hunt up *The Ring and the Book* now if I particularly desired: but of course I did not insist.

Indeed, I had already been beguiled by the poet's cordial manner into staying much longer than I ought, and I soon took my leave.

C. W. BARDEEN.

"row, and look at it again. If I don't write before Sunday, "come to lunch and I'll tell you about it." So I got up a subscription, and on his seventieth birthday, May 7, 1882, sent him a handsomely-bound set of his own Works in an oak case carved with Bells and Pomegranates, and with this inscription in the volumes: " To Robert Browning on his Seventieth Birthday, May "7, 1882, from some members of the Browning Societies of Lon- "don, Oxford, Cambridge, Bradford, Cheltenham, Cornell, and " Philadelphia, with heart-felt wishes for his long life and hap- " piness. These members having ascertained that the Works of "a great modern Poet are never in Robert Browning's house " when need is to refer to them, beg him to accept a set of these " Works, which they assure him will be found worthy of his most " serious attention."—Dr. F. J. Furnivall, president of the Browning Society of London, in " Pall Mall Budget " for Dec. 19, 1889.